A List-Less Life

By

Darcy Delany

A List-Less Life

If I build it, he will come.

My Dream Man

1. Dark hair.

2. Taller than me (logistics matter).

3. Wants a relationship and a family (rather than a fling, friends-with-benefits or variation of).

4. Isn't a cyclist or a triathlete (why are they all nuts? Besides, someone who is more worried about his calorie intake than me and who shaves his legs is too effeminate).

5. Has a job (failed businessmen trying to 'find themselves' need not apply. Do I look like an ATM?).

6. No Geminis – why do the ones I date always have a psycho personality as part of their twin nature?

Chapter One

Lists lead to success, Gina Trent had found.

After all, she'd used them to graduate with a law degree and organise her busy life. Why not use a list to find a man?

'He'd be perfect.' Gina prodded the photograph of Pierce Brosnan while the sounds of the local café hummed around her.

'He's a tailor's dummy. A nice clotheshorse, but couldn't handle a bar brawl,' said Alli, eyeing the waiter's bulging muscles.

'A brawler wouldn't be a good husband.' Gina followed Alli's gaze and smiled.

'You're thirty two, you've heaps of time. Remember, once you have a baby there'll be no more sleep-ins, and your body will be ruined.' Alli stabbed Gina's list with her finger. 'Better put plastic surgery on your list straight after the give birth entry.'

Gina rolled her eyes and refocused on her list.

'If I meet someone in the next six months and get married within eighteen months, I can have three kids by the time I'm thirty six.'

'Being organised is one thing, but where's the spontaneity? The magic? Romance doesn't happen on a schedule.'

Gina swallowed a mouthful of coffee. 'I tried going with the flow. Look how that's worked out.'

Alli laughed. 'Oh, don't stop now. Your dating disasters are my only entertainment.'

'Glad to be of help.' Gina winked.

'But you should go after men, not wait for them to come to you.'

'I can't chase them,' Gina said with a laugh. 'I'm still massaging calendula oil into the scars from my last collision with a garbage bin.'

Alli leaned her elbow on the table and propped her head on her palm. 'So you write a list of what you want in a man instead? Are you going to hand it to potential suitors before you meet them? Or will you advertise it in the paper and see who applies for the position?'

Gina chuckled. 'Why not?'

Gina removed the box hidden behind the winter woollies in her closet. Its pink covering with white dots had faded with time, the corners showing the cardboard content beneath the cheery facade. She sat on the bed and opened the lid in awed silence.

She forced herself to do this less often now, but there were times, like today, when the memories surged forward in a tidal, consuming rush.

Gina pulled out the small, white knitted bonnet she'd bought the day she'd miscarried her baby, and the tears she'd been holding in spilled down her cheeks.

How I could have doubted I wanted you? When she'd discovered her pregnancy, she'd written a list to decide whether to keep her baby. Pros on one side, cons on the other.

It made her stomach churn to think of what she'd written on the 'cons' side of the list. Her degree. Her career. Losing friends. Losing respect. Upsetting her parents. Difficulty finding a partner with a baby.

None of it seemed important now. Not after living without her.

She would have been nine now, if she'd lived; and Gina's house would have been filled with noise, rather than the silence broken only by the chatter of passers-by on the footpath outside. She'd have been driving her little girl to sport, dancing and school, rather than sitting and wondering what might have been.

I need your help little one, to get things right this time. Gina stroked the soft white wool and took a deep breath. 'I won't make the same mistake again, I promise you.'

Chapter Two

Gina groaned as her laptop bag landed with a thud on the footpath. *Why on earth did I walk back to the office with this lot?* She shifted her folder on to her hip and hefted the laptop bag up; grateful that Canberra's afternoon peak-hour hadn't begun. *At least there are fewer witnesses.* She needed time to decompress after the disastrous inter-departmental briefing, but the laptop now weighed more than it did when she started out—or so it seemed. Then the wind started, whipping long, dark brown strands of Gina's hair about her face; lashing at her eyes. At this rate, her eyes would be red rather than blue when she returned to work. Gina lifted her free hand to clear the offending hair when the laptop crashed down on her foot.

'Shit.' *Right on the toe.* Gina winced and pulled the bag from her shoe.

'No need to beat yourself up.'

Gina looked up to the face of a man-god. Piercing blue eyes with a smattering of smile lines, and dark brown hair being ruffled by the breeze. She stood and raked her eyes downward, resting on his well-defined arm muscles showing through rolled-up white shirtsleeves.

He looked like a young Pierce Brosnan from *Remington Steele*. And he had her at a disadvantage. Gina gulped and straightened her shoulders. 'You try walking in heels while keeping a dress down and carrying a pack mule's load.'

'I left my dress at home today, fortunately.' The man-god raised his eyebrows at her, his sparkling eyes and widening grin sending her stomach into a paroxysm of butterflies.

'I, um, have to get back to the office.'

'Hmm. The way you're going, that might be a few hours away,' the man-god replied. 'Here, let me walk you there. May I?' He nodded at her laptop bag.

The man-god's fresh-scented cologne filled her nostrils and she caught her breath. 'Sure. Thanks.' Maybe the afternoon would end well after all.

Back at her desk, Gina perused the card the man-god had given her, along with a tantalisingly soft peck on the cheek.

Alex Turner.

She leaned back in her chair and sighed, before touching her cheek where Alex had kissed her.

Yes, the spot still tingled. She *hadn't* dreamed it.

She looked down at the card once more.

He'd taken her number, and promised to call. But would he?

The other men she met were interested at first, then faded away, making her doubt she'd met them in the first place.

Alex may very well do the same.

Gina frowned as she noticed her unevenly filed thumbnail. She wouldn't blame him if he didn't call. Canberra was full of women who looked as if they'd stepped out of *Vogue*. Yet she always appeared ruffled, her nails didn't grow, and she didn't wear skinny jeans for fear of the dreaded muffin top effect they created.

She looked down at her navy dress, which nipped in at her waist and flared elegantly over her chair in soft crepe folds. Her long legs were stretched in front of her, her Mary-Jane heels with a small bow at the front making her smile.

She had olde-worlde glamour rather than model-chic. And she had sassiness that younger, perfect-looking girls lacked.

Gina smiled. *He will call. Stop doubting yourself. You're a catch.*

Why A Man Would Be Lucky To Have Me

1. I have a job.

2. I can hold a conversation about more than the contents of the latest girly magazine.

3. I look after myself (well, apart from constantly having a cut, bruise or other injury).

4. I'm determined (so I need a man who likes that . . .).

5. I'm strong (need to let the guys think I need them now and then, good for their ego. . .)

6. I'm organised (so I need a man who appreciates it. No 'go with the flow' types . . .).

Chapter Three

Gina walked as quickly to her boss's office as she could without marching, her heels clicking over the tiles of the kitchenette in angry taps. *Why hasn't Alex called?* her steps seemed to say, getting louder and heavier as her anger increased. She rounded the corner, her steps more like stomps. The fact her white collar criminal prosecution was not going forward only made her temper worse; but it was no way to arrive at the boss's door. Gina slowed, inhaled a deep breath, and tucked her pink silk blouse into her skirt before rounding the corner to where her boss, George, sat at his large oak desk. A kind-hearted man, he looked disconcertingly similar to Mr Magoo.

Gina knocked, and George raised his head and smiled.

'Gina. Everything all right?' He gestured for her to take a seat.

'No.' She sat in the chair, back straight. 'George, we have to continue with this Fedco case. I'm tired of watching cases go nowhere.'

George nodded. 'But we need to be realistic. We can't take cases forward if they don't have a chance of winning; it's a waste of resources.'

'I know. It's just that I hate seeing anyone get away with something they should be prosecuted for.'

'We don't have enough evidence for this case to stick. I'd prefer to focus on cases where we'll secure a conviction.' George smiled. 'You remind me of myself when I first started. I'm glad I've found one protégé before I retire.'

Gina laughed. 'Glad you think so.'

George leaned forward. 'Everything all right? You don't seem yourself.'

Gina bit her lip. George had an uncanny ability to know when she was upset and trying to hide it.

'I'm fine, George. Thanks.'

George peered at her for a few seconds. His inquisitor look. 'Be kinder to yourself. You've been working back every night.'

Gina sighed. 'I will.'

She walked back to her office, her steps slow and heavy. She'd read and re-read her list: *Why A Man Would Be Lucky To Have Me*, but it wasn't enough to quiet the negative voice in her head.

The sunlight dappled over her desk and flopped into her chair. *Chocolate.* Gina reached down to her drawer of chocolates, biscuits and chips. It was known as the 'magic drawer' in the office, given its resemblance to the bottomless bag carried by Mary Poppins. Her eye fell on a box of dark chocolates, and she turned the lid to show the options. 'Turkish delight or pineapple treasure?'

'Hmmm hmmm.'

Gina's head whipped up at the sound of someone clearing their throat. Alex leant against the door jamb, eyes dancing.

'I had a meeting nearby. Hope you don't mind.'

He heard me talking to myself. Great. She coughed. 'Bad day.'

'So I see. Me too.'

Gina's breath slowed with anticipation as he walked over to her desk and took the chocolate box lid out of her hands. A jolt shot up her arm as his fingertips brushed against hers. She swallowed and looked up at him.

'Care to join me for something stronger?'

Chapter Four

Gina played with the stem of her martini glass. 'Want another one?' Alex nodded at the empty glass in her hand.

'No, thank you.' Thoughts of work had faded with the last remnants of daylight, and the hypnotic dance of tea lights bounced off the window near their table. She needed no more stimulation; just sitting across the table from Alex sent her senses zinging. One minute she was relaxed, the next, so tense she wanted to pounce at him over the table. It had been a long time since someone had made her feel this way, and it was a feeling she could get used to.

'You really care about your work, don't you?'

Gina smiled and focused on Alex's face. He'd been a perfect gentleman so far, letting her choose where to go, holding her chair out for her, and jocularising her from her work-induced funk. *Don't overanalyse. Just enjoy yourself.*

'Plenty of people hate what they do. But you, you have a . . . radiance. A passion.'

Gina's heart pounded and she let go of the martini glass.

'It's very attractive.' Alex leaned over and covered her hand with his. Their eyes locked.

I want you, but can I trust you? His hand was warm and reassuring, but the way his thumb stroked Gina's fingers gave her shivers. It was time to jump.

'Walk?'

Gina squeezed Alex's hand and nodded. It was worth taking the risk.

***

'So was it as good as you imagined?' Alli asked, leaning over the table.

'Better,' Gina whispered, raising her eyebrows with a smile.

'You lucky thing. Does he have a brother?'

Gina shook her head. 'No. Only child.'

'Just my luck,' Alli said with a sigh.

No, just my luck, Gina thought, a small smile playing on her lips. It had been worth the risk, all right. Alex had cooked breakfast for her, despite only having two hours' sleep. He was planning to cook dinner for her tonight – if they got that far. She grinned.

'Oh stop with the flashbacks! I can see exactly what you're thinking about!' Alli sat back in her chair.

'Sorry.' Gina looked at the table, her face hot.

'Don't be. I'm glad to see you happy.'

Gina nodded, despite the tightening in her chest.

'Gee, don't look so cheerful.' Alli raised an eyebrow at her.

'Don't mind me, just thinking about work again.' She gave as broad a smile as she could. 'Hard to break old habits.'

'Stop worrying so much. It will all work out fine. Stop overanalysing.' Alli shook her head before her eyes lingered on the torso of a passing waiter.

Gina bit her lip. *If only it was so easy.*

Chapter Five

'Working over the weekend again?' Alex kissed her on the cheek on his way to her kitchen sink, coffee cup in hand. Gina loved their Sundays, spent at his house one week and hers the next. She loved seeing how Alex blended into her home and her life, as if he had always been there. After three months of dating she was still waiting for the catch, but instead of things going wrong, they kept going right. And it made her nervous.

'I have to; I'm in court tomorrow and got nothing done on Friday with the compulsory training day.'

Alex laughed. 'Ah the joys. Makes me feel better volunteering for the crisis team, though.' Since she'd been dating Alex, it seemed that the Department of Foreign Affairs experienced a crisis a month, but his weekend absences relieved her guilt about her own weekend workload. Usually, men didn't understand, and either left to find someone else who was available when they wanted company, or drifted away, never to call again.

But not Alex.

He came up behind her and put his hands on her shoulders, kneading the muscles of their tension. Gina groaned with relief. 'That is fantastic.' She glanced at the mantel, smiling at the bunch of red roses in her favourite crystal vase. He sent her a bunch a week, much to the envy of her work colleagues.

'You can leave them at work, you know.'

Gina turned to face him. 'I know. But I like seeing them. They remind me of you.' Her eyes were moist, and she blinked to keep back the tears.

Alex bent and kissed her. 'I'm not going anywhere. You know that, right?' The bench creaked as he sat down beside her and put his arm around her. He smelled of eggs, bacon, and soap. How did he make plain soap smell so – sexy? Her mouth watered as she breathed him in.

'You better not go anywhere.' She pushed her fears away as his lips met hers.

It's not just lust. Lust doesn't look after you when you have the flu, cook dinner for you when you have a horrible day at work, or do the vacuuming so you can soak in the tub a little longer. And lust doesn't look at you with eyes which look teary at times as they tuck a lock of hair behind your ear. Or hold you like you're a precious piece of china.

Love had seemed so different on paper. She hadn't been prepared for the constant sense of hunger for a word, a look, a touch. And it wasn't just for the physical things, but that feeling of being seen, and heard, and loved for it all; good and bad.

Her fears were easing to the point she'd even looked at rings. *Those rings.* She even tried one on the other day. And it felt – almost real.

Chapter Six

Thailand was surreal for Sean Tate. Instead of unpacking engagement presents, he packed his now ex-girlfriend's possessions in a box, labelling it with a bold black marker. She should be here with him, not married to another man. When had she planned to tell him? How long had everyone else known? Not that he had the energy to be angry; he was busy picking up his shattered dreams from the floor. Sean closed his eyes, imagining the gossiping back home of colleagues who knew them both and had watched as the romance with Leigh's now husband developed.

Her chosen was sophisticated, older, richer, but dragged enough baggage with him to fill the Orient Express. Sean contemplated his own meagre bank balance, the small car he'd owned since his teens (scrapped before his first diplomatic posting), and the wardrobe full of shorts, T-shirts and pairs of thongs. Leigh always said she found his simple lifestyle 'refreshing'.

What signs did I miss? Sean wondered as he worked through his apartment, removing mementoes of her from bookshelves, photo frames and cupboards. Perhaps she'd been right, maybe he did only see what he wanted to. And what he'd wanted to see was that Leigh loved him as much as he loved her.

He ran his hand over his chin and felt the stubble that had accumulated since he'd heard. No point shaving without someone to stay looking good for.

Is there a prescription to remove rose-coloured

glasses? Sean wondered as he piled the collection into the bin. *Because until there is, I'm done.* It wasn't the first time he'd been hoodwinked by a woman who promised him a future, then whisked it away.

And he was done being amiable about it.

No more long-distance romances, either, he reminded himself.

His heart was hopeful, but not strong enough to withstand this again.

'Thank goodness that's over.' Gina rocked forward to get out of the seat. After hours of driving, she was stuck in a seated position.

Alex hopped out of his seat. 'Here, let me pull you out.'

Gina waited until he was beside her, enjoying the sensation of the muscles in his forearms flexing as he helped her. 'I feel like an oyster being prised out of a shell.'

Alex leant in and pulled out her handbag. 'I prefer you to an oyster any day.' He leaned again to kiss her, their lips touching gently. The slowness of the long-weekend traffic had, for once, not bothering her. Alex actually made it fun, making up crazy stories and playing his own version of I Spy. *Does this man have any bad qualities?* He viewed her clumsiness as cute and considered her to be hot even when she was in her flannel pyjamas. *And, he likes kids.* Gina thought of the copy of *The Baby Manual* and a stash of nursery rhyme CDs which were on her hall table. Finally, she was daring to dream. But in isolation.

She looked up. It wouldn't be a secret for long. Alex was striding to the door, and in seconds he would see her hall table and its contents.

'Hon, would you check the boot please? I heard a rattle as we were driving home.' She marched past a frowning Alex, heart thumping as she bolted into the hall, grabbed the CDs and started stuffing them into the hall cupboard.

'Good view.' Alex came up behind her and circled her waist in his arms, his voice almost a purr.

Gina jumped, and the CDs clattered to the floor. He leant down and picked up a CD, and held it in front of him. *Classical lullabies.*

'Umm . . . something you want to tell me?'

She looked up at his face, which was registering a range of emotions gauging from the twitching lips and reddening ears.

'It's not what you think.'

'So you want to be engaged in a year, married and pregnant the next, and have three kids by the time you're thirty six?' Alex scratched his chin. 'Not that there's anything wrong with that. Ten points for having goals, babe,' he said, reaching out and squeezing her hand. 'But when does the one year mark get measured from? Our first date, or the first time we . . .'

'From the time we agree.' She looked up at him, lips pursed in what she hoped was a look of determination, but a smile was curling at the edge of Alex's mouth.

'You drive a hard bargain; ring first.' Alex looked into her eyes, his smile widening.

Gina fiddled with the silky material of her skirt with her free hand, the folds of which clung to her perspiring legs. *He'll run now, for sure. I was so close, and now, because of one mistake, it's all over. Oh crap.*

'Well, let's see how we go, shall we?' Alex took her hand from her skirt, and clasped it in his.

Gina looked up at him, hardly daring to believe what she'd heard. 'So you don't think it's crazy?' Metaphorical butterflies flitted in her stomach.

'No, babe, it's what I would do if I were in your shoes.' Alex gave a low laugh and leaned in to kiss her.

***

The café owner, Marta, set down their orders and smiled. 'Good to see you eating properly, Gina.' Another woman determined to feed her, but this time, she didn't mind. Soon, she might be eating for two, and that filled her with an appetite for food and life that she'd not realised was missing. Until now.

Gina grinned. 'I can't resist your cooking, Marta.'

Marta rolled her eyes and grinned before walking away.

'He sent me the most gorgeous box of red roses to work,' Gina said, stirring her coffee with gusto. Alli reached out with a napkin and mopped up the coffee that spilled out.

'I thought it was over when I told him about the plan,' Gina said, slopping her spoon on to the table and spilling even more coffee, 'but he's been all over me. He's even taking me out to view houses. Not for us to buy together, it's for him, but he has set up an online account so I can pick the places we'll visit by setting up a filter, and it creates an automatic list with times and everything.' Gina's hand waved in excited spirals. She'd been grinning constantly since they'd talked, and floated rather than walked.

'Play it cool. Just because he didn't run a mile when you first told him about the plan, doesn't mean he'll stay comfortable with it. Follow his lead – and don't get all officious with him.'

Gina frowned.

'I know you – you'll be holding quarterly review meetings.'

'I will not.' Gina's cheeks flushed. She had thought about revisiting their conversation in a few months if Alex hadn't progressed their relationship. She sighed. Alli was right – she had to slow down before she scared Alex away. She'd scared men away before.

But it was hard to stay calm when the dreams she'd nurtured for so long were within reach. *It's happening. Really happening.* Just that morning she'd cut out pictures from *Mum To Be* and stuck them in her diary. Just in case she needed them.

A smile played on her lips. She'd not had the courage to even look at a baby magazine before. And now . . . her luck was changing.

Chapter Seven

Gina put the knife beside the pile of julienned carrots, her temper rising. 'But we made plans. We never go out, you're always working. And the one time we plan something . . .' She walked away from Alex's kitchen bench and sat down at the dining table, its glass top smudged with fingerprints. Not that Alex cared about such things. Still, they irked her, not because it looked messy, but because he'd purchased the table without talking to her first. Not something a man did if he was planning on asking his girlfriend to marry him.

Alex sat beside her, taking her hands in his. 'Hey. I don't like this any more than you do. But it will help me get that posting, and then you can focus on something other than work.' He stroked her cheek, his eyes searching hers. I'm doing it for us.'

'I know.' Gina sighed. 'But we hardly see each other.' Although their relationship had been progressing, the longer she waited for a proposal, the more stressed she became.

She kissed Alex on the cheek and stood up, heading back to the bench and the pile of carrots, hoping the mundane action of chopping vegetables might soothe her shifting thoughts.

'The good things in life require sacrifice, Gina,' Alex said. 'But it will be worth it.'

Gina picked up another carrot, her eyes blurry with tears. She commenced her slicing; but her eyes looked beyond the chopping board, seeing the plans she had for their weekend away, and the next thing she felt was the knife slicing the edge of her thumb.

'Ouch!' The knife clattered to the bench, and she reached over and turned the cold tap on. She let the tears flow as the soothing stream of water mingled with the red streaks of blood in the sink. It was pointless arguing with Alex, he had to work if he was asked. She would expect him to support her if the situation were reversed. *What's wrong with me?*

Alex walked over to the sink. 'It's just a surface cut; it will be fine with a Band-Aid or two.' He turned off the tap. 'Here, hold the skin together. I'll get the antiseptic and Band-Aids.'

Gina nodded, grateful that at least one of them remained calm, and pressed the skin on either side of the cut together.

'I'll make it up to you. I'll take you out for a late dinner tomorrow, okay? Would you like to try that new Nepalese place?'

She winced as he dabbed the antiseptic over the cut. 'You laughed when I mentioned it.' Gina raised her eyebrows, not ready to forgive but happy to call a truce, for now.

'Book it for seven tomorrow.' Alex stretched a Band-Aid over her thumb, before putting it to his lips and kissing it.

At 8:30 the following night, Gina threw her clutch on to the bed and let her tears flow. No matter if her make-up ran now. She kicked her heels off, one hitting the wall before bouncing to the floor. *Just like any plans I make with him*, she thought as she looked at it.

Chapter Eight

'Gina, I'm worried about you,' her mother whispered.

Gina pursed her lips and stared at her parents' kitchen table, garishly clad in a green and red crochet tablecloth. Since retiring, her mother had created enough crocheted items for her own house as well as her children's. Gina's tablecloths remained in the linen closet, unused, except for the times her parents visited.

'I know.' Her voice came out in a squeak.

'Last week you gashed your arm in the garden, this week you have a thumb covered in Band-Aids.'

'I'm just working too hard.' Gina closed her eyes and leaned against the back of the wooden chair. It was just the right height for her to lean her head back and stretch her neck, which was tighter than usual. Alex had been working late all week, and she'd missed his neck massages.

'You *are* working too hard. No relationship should be this difficult.' Her mother clinked the plates.

Gina opened her eyes. 'Mum, we know what we're doing. We can't afford for me to stay at home with children here in Australia. He needs to get a posting first, then I can have children while taking a career break.' Her stomach clenched as she listened to the words. *If only I could believe it.*

Her mother shook her head. 'There's nothing stopping him from proposing now.'

There was no point arguing with her mother, who was only saying what she herself had thought many times this year. And when their one-year anniversary had passed with no proposal, her earlier fears had returned. Gina stood. 'I'll be late, Alex is coming over for dinner.' Gina kissed her mother, who enveloped her in a hug.

She wished it made her feel safe, like it used to when she was a child. But it only reminded her of what she didn't have with Alex.

Security.

'Gina?' Alex called as the front door closed hours later.

'I'm in here.' Gina shoved her feet in her fluffy rabbit slippers and stood up, pulling her dressing gown around her. *He should have been here hours ago.* She padded out to the hall to give Alex a kiss. Regardless of how things were between them, she was determined to make an effort. All couples had bumpy sections in their relationship; the important thing was to think positive and get through them.

'Hi.' Alex stood in the doorway to the lounge room, twisting his car key around in his fingers.

Gina's chest tightened as she watched him. Usually he would throw his keys on the coffee table and settle himself on the couch beside her.

'What is it?' She stood on the spot, unnerved by the palpable sense of dread hanging in the air between them.

'Something happened at work today.'

Gina's heart pounded in her chest. 'Okay.' She looked at Alex's hand, the finger tips were turning white as he gripped the key.

'I think we should sit down.'

Gina nodded and headed for the lounge, her heart sinking as Alex's footsteps trod sullenly behind her.

'What is it?' Gina sat on the couch and patted the empty sofa cushion. Alex put his key on the side table and sat beside her, taking her in his arms. He said nothing for a moment, but stroked her hair.

'You know how we talked about you coming with me on posting?'

Gina stiffened. 'Yes.'

'I've been given a posting to Port Moresby. But— I'm going unaccompanied.'

Gina pulled away. 'You're what?' Her chest heaved as glared at him. *It can't be true. I'm not hearing right.*

Alex's shoulders sagged. 'I'm sorry.'

This isn't happening. This can't be happening. What the hell is going on?

'I know it's a big step to go on a posting together.' Gina's chin wobbled as she searched Alex's face for a sign of hope.

'I'm so sorry. I can't give you what you want yet. I'm not ready.' He rushed out of the room, slamming the door behind him. Its echo was the last sound she heard before bursting into tears.

What I Can Do To Get Alex Back

1. Wait and hope (chances of success: 0).

2. Find someone else (unlikely, since I can't stop crying and have bruises all over from running into things as a result).

3. Do something (better. But what – revenge? No, that's for psychos. Win him back? Possible if I was a Glamazon girl. But then, it's not all about looks, is it?).

Chapter Nine

Gina threw the crumb-sprinkled blanket off herself and stumbled to the window. Pulling back a corner of the curtain, she peeked out the window and winced as the sunlight hit her eyes.

What is Alex doing? Stumbling back from a night out? Or waking up with another woman beside him? Gina's tortured mind had imagined many scenarios, all of which involved the cruel taunting of her inner critic. *No wonder he left, you're too clingy. You should have been more independent. You should have . . . should, should, should.*

Gina dragged herself into the bathroom to dress, her legs heavy. She had stayed awake until 2:00 a.m. watching one movie after another, wrapped in a dressing gown and covered with the crocheted blanket her mother had given her last Christmas. Somewhere between *Sense and Sensibility* and *Persuasion,* Gina realised that the break-up could be a mere detour from the plan. Just like Elinor and Edward's. And Anne and Frederick's. This didn't need to be the end, but it was up to her to get her plan on track again. She peered into the mirror, gasping at her matted hair and the crumb flakes that clung to her eyelashes. The effect was that of a startled bird, which wouldn't do at all if she was to get her plan moving forward once more. Gina lifted her chin. She had to get back in control of her life, and that meant no more sulking.

She headed to the shower, flicked on the mixer tap and let the water warm. *I wonder what he's doing now.* Gina slammed the shower door shut and let the water run over her, trying to hold back tears. *Is he with someone else? Having fun, while I'm here* . . . She squirted a glob of shampoo on to her hand and rubbed it into her hair with gusto. *Stop it. That won't help.* But still the negative thoughts came: images of Alex laughing with someone else, Alex proposing to someone else . . . *No, that won't do.* She closed her eyes and rinsed out the shampoo, shoulders sagging. It would be easy to go back to the sofa and lose herself in her grief. But she'd made a promise to the baby she'd lost.

Hair rinsed, Gina opened her eyes. *I told you I wouldn't let you down, and I won't.*

'So how are you? Alli nursed her coffee cup between both hands, squinting at Gina through the afternoon sun.

'Better. Because I'm going to win him back.' Just saying the words made her feel powerful again, and the pain in her chest subsided.

Alli put down her coffee cup and frowned.

'Gina, are you mad? You are well rid of him. How could he up and leave you like that?' Alli shook her head.

Gina's chest tightened. 'Because he was scared. I was hunting him down like a poor rabbit. Any man would have done the same thing.'

Alli shook her head. 'I think he was just gutless.'

'Maybe. But I love him, and I know he loves me. He will be a good husband. I think that all he needs is to learn just how much he misses me so he can overcome his fear.'

She'd told herself this so many times that she even believed it, now. Her inner critic told her she was being silly, that he was gone for good, and that she was wasting her time. But she would respond with positive affirmations like 'It's just my lack of confidence talking.' But every time she did so, a knot formed in her stomach.

A knot she didn't want to acknowledge.

'I have to at least try.' Gina's voice was small.

Alli sighed and shook her head. 'Sometimes I wish you weren't so stubborn.'

Why Working In The Public Service Takes Your Mind Off Having Your Heart Broken

1. It takes a long time to do the simple things, so you transfer your frustration on to bureaucracy rather than your ex.

2. The Dilbert-esque antics of your fellow bureaucrats will make you smile, even when you never thought you'd smile again.

3. Shredding documents for security purposes is cathartic – just imagine it's the ex.

4. The public service makes little sense at times, just like your previous relationship.

Chapter Ten

Cleaning out her office had seemed like a good way to deal with her pain, but trying to remove an old painting from her office was pushing her patience beyond its limits.

'Now, Ms Trent, fill out this form, fax it to this number, and you will get a call with a cost to remove the items.' Ned, the admin assistant, tapped his pen on the form.

'Why am I being asked to pay? Don't our maintenance staff already get paid?'

Ned shrugged. 'Not in their agreement. Asset disposal is a fee-for-service activity now.'

Gina groaned. 'Honestly. I might as well throw it in the skip myself.'

'No, you can't do that without filling out an asset disposal form and having the work health and safety folk sign off on it. If you don't, you could be in trouble come asset audit time. That said, what I don't know . . .' Ned cast a furtive glance down the hall.

'Got it.' Gina winked, taking the form and a Mars Bar from Ned's latest fundraising chocolate box. She needed something to ease the pain of this administrative melodrama. Back at her desk, she eased herself into her chair and peeled back the chocolate wrapper, hoovering up the pieces so quickly the wrapper was empty when she next looked down. *No matter, this is the best bit.* Gina ripped open the wrapper and picked up the tiny flakes of chocolate left behind. *The tinier the piece of chocolate, the better it tastes.* She licked her finger to pick up the remaining pieces, leaning over the wrapper with intense concentration.

'Gina, may I interrupt?' George's cheek dimpled as he smiled at her.

Gina gave a dejected look at the chocolate flakes sitting on the waxy white plastic and put the wrapper in the bin. 'Of course. Three o'clock sugar hit, you know.'

George sat in the chair opposite. 'I've just had mine. Although it was made with some sort of artificial sweetener. I'm supposedly consuming too much sugar.' He sighed as he looked at the wrapper.

'You wanted to talk to me about something?'

George tore his gaze away from the wrapper. 'Ah, yes.' He cleared his throat and frowned. 'Do you remember the senior legal adviser role we filled earlier this year in Papua New Guinea?'

Gina sighed. 'Yes. The one that you sent the Sydney barrister to fill?' She was considered for that job, but it went to someone from the old boys' network instead. She raised her eyebrows, hoping George sensed her anger, but he merely stared at her and touched his chin.

'You have a little something.'

Gina wiped her chin and cleared her throat to signal to George to continue.

'Yes, now our candidate left the role unexpectedly. And we wondered whether you would still be interested?'

Gina's mouth fell open. *PNG. Alex is in PNG. He'll have to change his mind when I'm there.* She grinned. *I'll only be a few months off track with my plan.*

Alli would think she was crazy. But this was her chance.

Gina nodded. 'I'll go.'

Chapter Eleven

Later that night, Gina groaned as the phone rang. 'Just when I get in the shower.' She turned off the tap, pulled the towel from the rail and wrapped it around her as she bolted for the ringing phone, muttering as the draught curled its way around her. She should have been living in the well-insulated, double-glazed windowed family home she and Alex picked out rather than freezing in this uninsulated old place.

She picked up the phone. 'Hi.'

Gina dropped the towel. Alex.

She swallowed. First the job in PNG, now this. It was a sign.

Gina reached down and hoisted the towel over her with one hand, landing it on her shoulder. She wriggled it towards the other side of her back. 'Come on,' she muttered.

'You sound busy. Have I called at a bad time?'

'No! I mean, I was just picking something up. It's fine. I'm fine. Things are fine. In answer to your question.' She closed her eyes and shook her head. *Stop babbling. Think Scarlett. Haughty, confident and never backed into a corner.* She cleared her throat. 'And how are things with you?'

'Good. Hot here, though.'

Gina rolled her eyes. This was painful. He'd be off the phone in seconds if she didn't inject some excitement. 'I can imagine. I'm glad you called, as I have good news. I'm taking that job in Port Moresby I missed out on last time.' Silence. Gina bit her lip. 'Yes, I'll be there in a month.

Perhaps I'll see you around, once I'm settled.' Still nothing. 'Alex?'

'Oh. Well, that's great.' Alex cleared his throat. 'I'm happy for you.' He laughed. 'You'll be earning more than me.'

'Really?' Gina's heart lightened. He sounded happy for her. And he had called her, so he clearly missed her.

The plan was falling back into place. Now all she had to do was keep up her charade: if Alex thought she didn't miss him, then he'd be curious why. It would make him think about her endlessly until she arrived, and their reunion would just be a matter of time. But she had to keep him off-balance. The old Gina would have waited on the phone, hoping for him to beg her for a second chance. She had to show him that things had changed. 'Well, thanks for calling, must run. Just on the way out for a drink.' She tried not to laugh.

'Oh. Oh, sure. Bye then.'

'Bye, thanks for the call.' Gina made sure the call had ended before she did let out a laugh.

It's working. She grinned at the phone in her hand.

Chapter Twelve

Four months later, Gina soaked up the sparkling aquamarine brilliance of Port Moresby harbour as she drove to work. It had taken her days to feel confident driving on her own; the heavy, chaotic traffic a world apart from the organised Canberra roads she had left behind. And that wasn't the only difference: if she had an accident here, her safety was in danger from the other drivers. She bit her lip. She could only hope she never faced that situation.

Cars with handwritten number plates and windows constructed from sticky tape and plastic whizzed past her, the occupant of one leaving hers covered in a stream of red-coloured spittle. 'Ugh,' she muttered, flicking on the windscreen wipers to remove the spatters that bounced off the bonnet. She'd heard about betelnut, the locals' vice of choice. *If only it didn't look so much like blood,* she thought with a grimace.

A man walked down the street with a long-bladed bush knife, and she stiffened in her seat. She was about to check her doors were locked when the man raised the knife in a wave, flashing red-stained teeth at her. She grinned and gave a small wave in response, her smile fading when she noticed the toddler beside him, a mini pack of Twisties in one hand and his father's hand in the other. The proximity of a weapon and a baby made her shiver, but as she drove on, the scene was repeated. In some cases, babies were carried in string bags, the straps around the adult's forehead. *A very different view of safety, here,* she thought, before smiling. *Ned would not approve.*

The road curved past the Harbour City shopping centre, a trail of cars that had seen better times emitting exhaust fumes of varying colour. An overcrowded bus billowing smoke chugged past her, a man hanging on to the frame of the open back door glaring at her. No wonder. She had a new, air conditioned car, and the locals had to make do with that. As she turned into the gates of her office, she hoped her new colleagues would receive her more warmly.

She stopped the car under a rain tree and took a deep breath. The legal office was in an old fibro-clad building with a veranda running across the front. *Just like my kindergarten*, Gina thought with a smile. The coincidence had to be a good sign.

With a skittering heart, she got out of her seat and pulled out her backpack from the boot. Not her usual choice for a work bag, but in addition to her laptop, she had to carry any drinking water she needed for the day, all of her food, and a supply of toilet paper. Gina glanced at the building as she heaved the laptop on to her back. *Here goes.*

She waddled towards the office, smiling at the men and women who watched her in silence from windows. She couldn't show them she was nervous.

It was then that she stubbed her toe on an uneven part of footpath, the heavy backpack hurtling her forward. Gina reached out to break her fall, which loosened her bag from her shoulders, sending it landing on the ground with an ominous thud.

What an entrance. Gina looked up.

No one moved, except a gardener who had been clipping bushes nearby. He put down his shears and picked up her backpack as she stood. 'Here missus.' He picked up the bag and held it out to her, his eyes narrowed.

Gina couldn't help smiling back. At least someone was treating her like a real person, not a character on a TV screen to be watched from afar.

'Thank you so much. I'm Gina, by the way.' She smiled and thrust out a palm covered with small pebbles and cement dust.

'Yom,' he said with a nod.

If Ned knew that Gina's office had rotten floor boards that trapped her heels, he would have demanded she fill in an occupational health and safety report. So when she called to order more equipment, she reminded herself not to mention that, or the fact that the offices were filled floor-to-ceiling with precariously stacked computer printouts. Best not to mention the need to clean the rat droppings from her desk each morning, either. She couldn't resist, however, telling him the reason she needed a new keyboard so soon.

'Ants,' she said, trying not to laugh.

'Huh? Ants don't eat keyboards?'

'These ones do. They love lights and even go into the kettle. I found a ball of them in the kettle water recently. That explained why I was getting ants in my tea – and I presumed it was the tea bags.'

'Hmmh. Well, I'll just put wear and tear down on the requisition form then.'

Gina put down the phone and looked out her office window. A fire had been lit to burn the day's rubbish, and the acrid smell of burning plastic reached her nostrils. That was one health and safety issue that did bother her. She coughed, and headed to the windows to shut the glass louvres against the acrid smoke that was now blowing in her direction.

Despite the conditions, Gina had come to love her office, and her work. Port Moresby was starting to feel more like home, except for one thing: Alex had still not called.

At first she'd pondered reasons to call him and help their reunion along, but her growing delight in her work and the local people made her pause.

She looked towards the jungle-clad Owen Stanley ranges and smiled. Somehow, in this unusual place, she was finding her strength.

The laughter of children from the road drew her out to the veranda. Children passed the offices each day on their way to and from the local school. *I would have had a child just about their age if I had – but don't think about that now.* She waved at a group of children who giggled and pointed at her. She was still a novelty to many, but she reasoned, at least they were interested in a good way.

The group stopped, picked up some rocks and threw them at a mango tree, sending green mangoes falling to the ground at their feet. 'Yayyy,' they cheered, scooping them up as a mangy dog ambled up to them.

'Rausim,' yelled one of the children. Another picked up a rock and threw it at the dog, earning laughter from his friends.

Gina raced from the veranda, earning curious stares from those she dashed past. Mangy dogs were not viewed highly by her local colleagues. 'Stop!' Would you like me to throw rocks at you?' she said, panting as she reached the group.

The children exchanged guilty glances.

'If I catch you again, I will send Yom after you.' The children stared at her, eyes large. 'But, if you walk past every day and don't throw things at the dogs, then on Fridays, you come to my office and I will give you some Twisties.'

They smiled. 'Bye missus.' The dog loped away now, and the children, distracted by the promise of Twisties, ran off, giggling.

Gina laughed as she watched them, buoyed by their happiness. They had less than children did back home, but they seemed happier. In fact, most people she worked with seemed happier.

No wonder I feel so good here, Gina thought with a smile.

Chapter Thirteen

Sean switched off his phone and turned on the television. Despite the balmy tropical temperatures and constant sunshine, his skin bore the pallor of a person enduring a Nordic winter. *Nordic winter – the state of my love life.* He closed the DVD player and settled on the sofa for another box-set marathon. *If Leigh had only told me what the problem was, I could have fixed it. Leigh knew I would have done anything for her.*

Didn't she?

He pressed play on the remote, thinking through all the things he'd said and done to show Leigh how much she meant to him. She wanted to live overseas, so he'd worked hard to secure this posting. She wanted to get engaged, so he'd bought her the ring she'd wanted. Still, none of it was enough.

What should I have done then? He stopped the DVD and frowned at the screen. Leigh had insisted on staying in Australia until she finished her projects. Should he have urged her to come with him regardless? He shook his head. No. He'd never jeopardise her career.

The truth was, no matter what he did, *he* was not enough.

Perhaps I should just sleep around like the other guys, and not worry about a relationship. He tried to imagine himself surrounded by giggling women hanging on his witty repartee and fighting amongst themselves to be near him. He grunted. That fantasy belonged to a confident man and he was far from confident now.

Besides, he was too old fashioned for flings.

He glanced at the laptop lying dormant on the coffee table. His friends had encouraged him to try online dating, and despite his fears, he'd found a service that seemed genuine. But every time he got to the sign-up page, he sat, staring at his blinking screen as he wondered who would want him.

His mates would say he was a coward, but it was more than that. He wanted to fall in love the traditional way: meet a woman, become besotted with her and sweep her off her feet.

Perhaps he was a coward, but he was also a romantic. And he wasn't ready to settle for anything less than romance just yet.

Sean looked back at the TV and turned the DVD back on.

This reminds me so much of Melrose Place, thought Gina as she drove into the compound for her diving lesson. A gardener clipped the grass with his bush knife, catching the pavers with a steady 'click', while another man swished at leaves with a coconut broom. Tropical birds called as a red sunset filled the sky. The hibiscus bushes, which were plentiful this morning, had been hacked back to mere sticks. She parked the car by the pool, looking up the driveway towards Alex's apartment building. The diving lessons she was taking were just her way of embracing the tropical way of life. They had nothing to do with getting closer to Alex, she reminded herself as she walked towards pool.

After the diving lesson, Gina pulled herself out of the pool and waved goodbye to the other students.
I did it, she thought, her lips curving into a smile. She glanced at the retreating backs of the other diving students, her heart sinking. No sign of Alex.

With a frustrated yank, she pulled her mask back from her forehead, yelping when the rubber band caught on her hair. 'You've got to be kidding.' She gave a gentle tug, wincing as her hair pulled at her scalp. Dislodging this would require a mirror.

'Need some help?' The voice was smooth, familiar, and bemused.

Gina's hands froze around the mask, her stomach leaping as Alex stepped in front of her.

She wanted to see him pale, thin, and heartbroken. Instead he looked tanned, healthy, and bemused.

He reached up, gently pulling the hair out of the mask, his familiar smell sending a flood of desire through her. Gina clenched her jaw. *He hurt me. He'll hurt me again if I let him.*

'That's a nice bruise you've got there. Let's get some ice on to it.' Alex put his hand on the small of her back.

'Sure,' she heard herself say, her mouth feeling suddenly dry.

Alex's apartment resembled a bachelor pad; ties littered the coffee table, empty glasses were strewn around, and unpacked boxes sat by the wall. Gina had imagined his apartment in her mind, but never expected something this . . . empty. She glanced around at the bare walls, the beige couch, and the drab brown rug. If they'd moved here together, she could have decorated the space. She clenched her jaw. *Don't think about that now.* But every step she took in his new home just reinforced her pain. He'd left her to live like this? He preferred this to being with her? Her heart beat faster in her chest.

'Sit down here, I'll be back in a minute.' Alex helped her on to the sofa and disappeared into the next room. She heard a door open and close, and the sound of ice crashing into something plastic. Frantic slamming of drawers followed.

Gina looked around the room again, her eyes falling on a stack of papers. With the sounds still emanating from the kitchen, she leant over and flicked through them. Emails. None to a woman, though. Gina put the papers back, heart now thudding.

'Don't worry; I'll take you round for a proper stickybeak later.' Alex held a face washer filled with what she guessed were ice cubes, a grin on his face. He jerked his head towards a mirror on the wall facing the kitchen and dining room.

Gina's cheeks burned, and she searched her mind for a witty retort.

But when Alex sat down next to her and his eyes locked with hers, her mind went blank. *Oh no, he's going to kiss me.* Gina caught her breath as his lips moved closer, jerking her head back as his lips touched hers.

'What's wrong?' Alex frowned and drew back.

Gina's stomach clenched. *I came here to get him back, but now I'm near him, all I can think about is when he'll hurt me again.* She bit her lip. 'I . . . can't,' she said, her voice small.

Alex's nostrils flared. 'Is there someone else?'

Gina glared at him, cheeks flushed with anger. 'Why do you care? You're the one who dumped me, remember?'

Alex took her hand. 'Why do you think I care?' He stroked her skin in slow, light touches which sent pulses of longing through her.

Gina swallowed. Talk about mixed signals. One minute she wanted to run from him, then the next . . . She pulled her hand away and folded her arms over her chest. 'I don't know what to think.'

Alex sighed. 'Gina, I know I should have handled things better. And I want to reconsider. What do you think, can we spend some time together, and see how we go?'

Gina narrowed her eyes at him. 'You need to earn my

trust again. So don't waste my time if you aren't prepared to do that.'

Alex raised his eyebrows, then nodded. 'Fair enough.'

Gina's heart slowed to a steady rhythm. 'Good.' She stood. 'I think it's best I leave now.'

Alex put the face washer on the sofa and jumped up from his seat. 'Would you like to have dinner? There's a lot to catch up on.'

Gina scanned his face. Small smile, eyes looking directly into hers. No hint of deception. Perhaps he meant what he said. 'Okay.'

Alex grinned. 'Great. I'll call you.'

When the Universe slams the door in your face, try the window.

Chapter Fourteen

Gina's new friend Kirsty Lawson had a luxurious apartment in the city, and a set of glamorous friends to match, it seemed. Gina looked down at her sarong as the noise of Kirsty's party whirled around her. *Who would have thought I'd need cocktail dresses in the tropics?* She bit her lip as she looked around at the array of designer dresses that now surrounded her. Still, she was out of the house, where she'd moped for two weeks, waiting for Alex to call. *It's a blessing in disguise that he didn't call,* she reminded herself. *And this is a chance to meet someone much better than him.* She breathed into her chest, willing her tense muscles to relax.

'Gina, you have to meet these two.' Kirsty had manoeuvred her to the edge of the balcony, where two women dressed in tank tops and sarongs stood against the backdrop of Ela beach. Gina's chest eased. *Some normally dressed people!*

'This is Jen, and her partner Vera.' Kirsty waved her hand and glass of champagne at the two ladies standing in front of her, before disappearing into the crowd. One had long, dark hair tied up in a ponytail, brown eyes twinkling with mischief. 'Hi, I'm Jen.'

Vera smiled. 'Vera. Nice to meet you.' Her blonde curly hair stood out like a halo around her.

'So, are you single?' Jen cocked an eyebrow.

'You can't ask her that straight away.' Vera shrugged her shoulders. 'Can't take her anywhere.' She smiled.

'I am, actually. Long story.' Gina took a sip of champagne.

'Really!' Jen moved closer. 'So, what happened?'

Jen gestured to a nearby couch and they sat. Telling her intimate personal secrets to strangers was not her usual approach, but there was something about Jen and Vera that made her trust them. Given her experience with Alex, she wasn't sure she should trust people so easily; but then he would have won, leaving her a victim.

Gina leaned back into the sofa's soft cushions, glancing over to the group of people now trying to limbo under a broomstick, with varying degrees of success. She should have been mingling more. Meeting new people. But here she was instead, about to confide her story to two strangers.

She looked into their eager faces and took a deep breath. She had to start trusting again sometime.

'You're too good for him,' Jen said once her story was over, passing her a pack of tissues from her bag.

Gina pulled one out and wiped her now running nose. 'I keep telling myself that. But then I think, if I'm so fabulous, then why did he leave me?' Her shoulders sagged as she leant her elbows on her thighs.

Vera laughed. 'Men are like kids going through McDonald's. They can't wait for dinner, which is much tastier – they want something now, and McDonald's smells good, looks good, but is full of crap. Much like the floozies I suspect Alex will go for,' Vera said.

Jen poured more wine into Gina's glass.

'I guess so,' Gina said with a shrug. 'But when will it happen?'

'Well, you need to give yourself more options,' Jen urged. 'And I know just how to do it – online dating.'

Jen pulled her phone out from her bag. 'It's super easy.' A few taps later, Jen held the phone out to her. 'Friends of ours used this site. It's not a candy store like the other sites. You pay to register, so the people on it are more likely to want a relationship. And you need to complete a personality profile with a hundred questions, so it's very thorough.'

'A hundred questions!'

'We'll help. Could be a bit of fun.' Vera winked.

Gina bit her lip. She'd almost stayed home tonight, but now she was glad she hadn't. And she'd thought she might meet a man – she'd done far better than that, she'd met friends who could help her find one anywhere in the world, according to a list the likes of which she had never imagined collating. Her mouth curved into a smile. 'Let's do it!'

Jen grinned. 'Okay – first question. What do you do when you are upset at someone?

'A. Vent.

'B. Punish them with silence.

'C. Tell them how you feel politely.

'D. Nothing.'

Gina sat back in her chair. 'Why is there no "all of the above"? I mean, each one applies in certain situations.'

'You can't say A, because it makes you sound out of control. B is a dead give-away someone has issues with confidence, as is D. C is the one to choose.'

An hour later, Gina's questionnaire was complete, and the tension she'd carried in her chest had eased. She'd actually been having fun, something she couldn't remember having since . . . she swallowed. She'd been so engrossed in her plan to get Alex back that she hadn't stopped to enjoy life, yet Port Moresby had, step by step, awakened her to the joy of living once more. One couldn't help being swept along in the energy of the people or the town, a feeling she hadn't experienced in the public-service town she'd left. She looked out over the lights bobbing in the harbour, breathing in the smell of the nag champa incense that wafted to her on the warm breeze. *Now I'm really living.*

'What name do you want to use?' Jen asked, interrupting her reverie.

'What about Lucy, as in *Lucy Sullivan Is Getting Married*? Hopefully I will be after doing this.'

'Lucy it is.' Jen tapped on the screen. 'Okay, let's see who you get.' A few seconds later, Gina's first matches came on the screen.

Jen laughed as she read the first profile. 'I'll call this one Mr Cleaver. Listen to this. "Must haves: I would like to start a family – ideally you would be between twenty-eight and thirty-two for this to happen. Must keep a clean and organised home."'

'Ooh, let me write back to him. "Dear Mr Cleaver. I clean with no clothes on."' Gina reached for the phone.

'Oh, and here we have Mr Creepy: "Please read carefully. I am looking for someone whose intellect and passion for the occult matches my own. To all the rest of you, there is someone else out there for you".'

'Scary, scary man. Next,' Gina cried, her enjoyment growing.

'This one's fantastic.' Jen pointed to the next match on the screen.

'Must haves: "Women should look like women, and since I dress like the classic men of Clark Gable's era, I am looking for my Vivien Leigh. Please don't contact me if you wear pants or thongs. Also, I follow a strict paleo diet, which you must be willing to follow." Gina burst out laughing.

A message request from the snappy dresser popped up on to the screen, and Jen typed back.

Hi there, thanks for your message. I am typing it to you in a swimsuit, tank top, sarong and flip flops, with, quelle horreur, no make-up or nail polish. Kiss kiss. Lucy.

Gina massaged her cheek muscles, which were now sore from laughing. Life without Alex was far better than she'd expected.

Chapter Fifteen

Gina took a sip of her drink and placed it on the coaster by her computer. Her new evening ritual included checking her online dating messages with a gin and tonic in hand, pacific music on a local radio station in the background. It was far more pleasant than shivering through a Canberra winter, and, she was surprised to find, far more pleasant than plotting to win Alex back. *To think of the time and energy I wasted trying to make him want me again, when I have men chasing me,* she thought with a smile, clicking open her latest online match.

At first she had gravitated to men who were similar to Alex, but a few conversations were enough to make her realise her mistake. All of them had either refused to commit to a time to talk on Skype, made plans to talk then changed them at the last minute without rescheduling, or they'd not been online to talk when planned. *Maybe now it's time to date someone different.*

Like Travis.

She glanced at her list. He wasn't a Gemini, nor a cyclist. But he *was* only thirty.

Gina's hand hovered over the mouse. She'd never dated anyone younger than her before, but she'd heard younger men liked dating older women, supposedly. And with the energy she had now, she felt thirty again.

She clicked over the 'accept request' button, and received an immediate response from Travis.

An hour later, she leaned back in her chair and peered at Travis's most recent message.

I live in Sweden but I'm in Thailand on holidays. Care to meet me? Separate rooms, of course.

Gina opened her web browser and typed in Travis's name. Facebook status: single. Yes, he lived in Sweden. Yes, his photos of Thailand were online. His LinkedIn accounts and Twitter matched all he'd told her.

She re-read Travis's message. *I've never been to Thailand. And I'm capable of looking after myself in a foreign country.*

With a shaking hand, she typed back to Travis. *Deal!*

Bookings made, she picked up the phone and dialled Jen's number. 'You won't believe what I'm about to do,' she said as soon as Jen answered.

'Don't you say hello anymore?' Jen asked.

'Oh stop pretending you're annoyed. Guess what? I'm meeting someone in Thailand.'

Instead of excited whoops of congratulation, Gina heard a muffled discussion and a scratching noise.

Jen still thought that rubbing the phone against her clothes was the equivalent of a mute button.

'Gina? It's Vera. Now, it's wonderful that you're getting back on the horse, but what do you know about this guy?'

Gina's cheeks reddened. 'I know enough, thank you very much.' She took in a sharp breath.

'Oh love, don't get upset with me. I'm just suspicious by nature.'

Gina sighed.

'I'm sure he's fabulous. But do me a favour and send me the details of your hotel, and anything you know about this guy. Oh, and get global roaming on your phone, so I can call you.'

Gina gave a soft laugh. She'd let Vera play Mum; it was the least she could do for all the dinners Vera had made her. And it couldn't hurt to be cautious. 'Okay, just for you.'

'Thanks love. I'll hand you back to Jen.'

'It's me again. Now that's sorted, let's talk about the important stuff,' Jen said.

In his apartment in Thailand, Sean Tate paused his DVD to check his beeping phone.

'Vera?' The last time he'd heard from Vera, she'd been determined to fly him to Port Moresby for a holiday, to 'shake him out of his doldrums'. Sean knew Vera's plans probably involved thrusting him in the path of eligible young women, so he'd avoided the trip by saying he was too busy with work. He opened the message, stomach clenching. Was Vera hassling him again?

Jen has created a monster. Damsel in distress coming your way. Will email photo and details of where she is staying, along with the likely cad she is meeting. Keep an eye on her for me? I owe you one. Vera.

Sean laughed. 'Nice try Vera, very smooth.' Then he opened the attachment, and his eyes widened at Gina's photo. *It seems I might owe you one, Vera.*

Chapter Sixteen

Sean watched Travis from his taxi and hated him instantly. A singlet top was not the attire in which to meet a woman for the first time. Gina seemed to agree, the fleeting look of disappointment on her face sending the blood coursing through his muscles. She deserved better than this shite.

He gave a wry grin. Gina's photo showed a beautiful, dark-haired woman with startling eyes, but in person, even from a distance, she radiated a feminine vulnerability he found himself drawn to. A woman he'd want to date; but here she was, seeing another man. Just his luck.

Travis helped Gina with her bags and their taxi pulled away.

'Follow them, but not too close.'

The driver nodded and pulled out after them. Lucky she'd arrived after peak hour, or they'd never have caught up to them.

A short drive later, they pulled up at the hotel, and Sean followed them at a discreet distance. He frowned as Sean led Gina straight to the bar after she checked in. *Bastard. He should have at least let her go and change.*

Sean stuffed down his growing anger enough to amble up to the bar, making sure not to attract their attention as they sat at a table.

The low music gave him the perfect ambience for eavesdropping while he pretended to be fascinated by his phone; if only he could stop sneaking glances at Gina. *She'll notice you staring, and then what?* But it became clear as she sipped her cocktail that Gina wasn't noticing him, or even Travis. Her yawns became so frequent that even Travis had to stop talking. Sean grunted to himself. *The man loved to talk. If only he had something interesting to talk about.*

'I need to go to bed, I'm sorry.' Gina stood, and Travis offered her a kiss on the cheek.

Sean sat, poised to follow them; but Travis sat down again, and Gina left for her room alone.

Bastard, Sean muttered. *Didn't even show her to her room.* Not that he'd wanted to think what might have happened if he had.

He scraped his chair back, ready to leave, when Travis picked up his drink and went to the bar. After a quiet word with the bartender, he left the bar, followed by a young boy.

Sean frowned. Something wasn't right.

He followed Travis, stopping at a nearby room and pretending to search his pockets for his key.

Out of the corner of his eye, he saw the boy follow Travis into the room.

Sean had left a tip with the porter, asking him to call him when the boy left the room. He'd headed home, planning to sleep, but fell into a fitful slumber on his couch instead.

It was early morning when the phone trilled.

'Mr? He not come out.'

Sean ran a hand through his hair, his mind churning through one awful possibility after another.

'Call the police.'

'Then I lose my job.'

'Okay, I'll call them. Thanks.' He ended the call and searched through his phone for his police contact's number.

***

'Thanks for your help.'

Sean nodded, then stared at the photo of Travis his police contact had given him. Travis Hughes – wanted for drug trafficking and the murder of a French tourist in Phuket. And possibly, that young boy who had gone into Travis's room.

'Sure, no worries mate.'

Sean sat down at his desk and dialled Gina's number.

No answer.

He clenched his fist. *If he's hurt her . . .*

Gina turned from her book and glared at Travis through her glasses. The windows had frosted up since the air conditioning was kept at Antarctic temperatures at his insistence. Gina wound her sole piece of warm clothing, a light cardigan, around her to keep out the intense cold. Instead of spending her first day in Thailand sightseeing, she had spent it in a hospital.

'You look like a librarian.' Travis laughed.

Better than looking like a piece of road kill. Gina surveyed his cuts and bruises.

'Great. You're awake.' Her voice was deadpan.

'Well I woke up because I'm in agony. Where's the nurse?' Travis grumbled.

'The nurse should be here soon to give you your next round of medication.' Gina lifted the glasses off and put them into their case. I'm going to the cafeteria.' *And going home after that*, she thought with relief.

Travis's youthful energy had seen him get into a fight at breakfast. She'd waited to see that he was alive and well – she'd have wanted the same from him if the situation were reversed. But now he'd woken up she wondered why she'd bothered. And if he thought he could be obnoxious and expect her to play nursemaid now, he had experienced more of a knock to the head than suspected.

Or he really was the giant ass he appeared to be. *A coffee; say goodbye to Dr Sree, he's been so kind; then out of here,* she reminded herself. *And when I get home, I'm adding 'must be over 35' to my list.*

'Yeah, would you get me a Hershey Bar? And when you come back, we can play doctors and nurses.'

The nurses had warned her that the medication could make him hallucinate, and if he thought she wanted to tend to his wounds, he really was hallucinating. 'You have plenty of nurses here, very good ones too,' she said, picking up her bag and walking out of the room.

The cafeteria had been her refuge. It served five-star food twenty-four hours a day, and she'd made numerous trips for comfort food while Travis had been sedated. Relief flooded through her as the sweet, gentle perfume of frangipanis wafted away the redolent smell of hospital antiseptic. *It will be over soon.*

She settled into a chair at the cafeteria before dialling Jen.

'Gina? It's Vera. Can you talk freely?' Vera's voice was high-pitched, unlike her timbre. It was a tone she only ever used when she was annoyed or upset; like when Jen didn't put a bin liner in the bin after emptying it. But there was something else in her voice, too- a hint of fear.

'Yes, I'm at the cafeteria. What's wrong?' Gina sat up, thoughts of Jen in hospital, or other disasters, racing through her mind.

'I've had a friend watching out for you while you've been in Bangkok. He's coming to see you now. Don't move until he gets there.'

'You've had someone watching me?' Gina asked, voice rising. Jen and Vera were like fun big sisters at best, and overbearing parents at worst.

'Sorry, I'm paranoid. I've seen it all in my stints with Immigration.' Vera's voice was quiet.

'Oh, I'll be glad to get home.' Gina's voice trembled. She'd misjudged Travis, just like she'd misjudged Alex. Only in this case, who knew what might have happened if Travis hadn't had his accident. She shuddered, despite the heat of the afternoon.

'And we'll be at the airport when you arrive, love. Hang in there. Sean is on his way.'

Thirty minutes later Gina looked up at the tanned face of the mysterious Sean. Divine hazel eyes, hazelnut-coloured hair, and light stubble around his chin. Butterflies danced in Gina's stomach. *He has an air of Bear Grylls' 'can do'.* She gave a small smile. She had someone to lean on now, and a good-looking someone at that.

'Drink?'

Gina nodded. 'Just a coffee though.'

Sean's taut backside disappeared into the café.

Nice form. Gina smiled, until her phone rang. Travis.

'Where have you been? I need you.'

'Don't call me again.' Gina ended the call and looked to see Sean's frowning face. 'That him?' he said, handing her a drink before sitting.

'Yes. What a right royal pain in the backside. Lucky the nurses find him funny; since they'll be the only ones caring for him once I go.'

Sean's eyes met hers, his mouth set firm. 'He won't have any nurses in the Thai prison system.'

The blood drained from Gina's head. 'What?' she said in a whisper.

'Travis is wanted for murder and drug trafficking. The police should be with him right about now.'

Tears blurred her eyes, and she played with the label of her ginger beer bottle. *I met up with a murderer. How could I get it so wrong?*

'You know what they say.' Sean nodded at her hands. 'Someone's deprived.'

Gina spluttered a half-laugh, half-cry, tears peeking out of her eyes. 'Well, given this week's events is it any wonder?' She brushed the tears with the back of her hand.

'Why don't I take you out for dinner?'

Gina looked up at him. His eyes were sparkling with enjoyment, and, maybe something else? *Can I trust him, though? I was so wrong about Travis.*

Sean leaned over the table. 'I know you're worried about trusting me. But Vera can vouch for me.'

Gina bit her lip.

'Here's my passport.' Sean reached into his pocket and pulled out the red-covered document. 'See? Sean Tate. Knight in shining armour, among other things.'

Gina took the passport and flipped it open to the photo page. It was him. She smiled as she looked at the photo. The same easy grin, the same dancing eyes. *I can trust him. I think.*

'Okay.' Gina looked up from the passport. 'But I'm keeping this until I get back to the hotel. Just in case.' Gina tucked the document into her bag.

Sean's eyebrows shot up. 'You do realise you look nothing like me. If you want to steal my identity you'll need a haircut, for starters.'

The suggestion was so unexpected that Gina burst out laughing. 'Touché.' She leaned back in her chair and beamed back at him, her fears replaced by a growing sense of excitement. 'You mentioned dinner?'

Gina sighed and tipped her head back as the warm night air blew over her. The sound of the water lapping against the side of the pier set a hypnotic rhythm for Sean's thoughts, as did the flickering candle on the table. The ever-present thoughts of Leigh had disappeared, replaced by a fascination with the woman sitting across from him, and who was now flipping her head back up and staring at him, face flushed and eyes bright. Completely unrestrained; and it wasn't just the drinks. She was fascinating to watch, every unfiltered gesture and thought was so removed from Leigh's controlled personality, he couldn't help but feel happy around her. And comfortable. There was no need to be on guard. She said everything that came to mind as it was. Good or bad.

'I looove the tropics.' Gina rested her head on one hand and grinned, making his heart swell.

'You really are a one-drink screamer, aren't you?'

'I didn't have lunch.' She stirred her empty glass with a bendy straw.

Sean clenched his jaw. The thought of Gina being hungry, or needing anything, made him fume. And while she was in his presence, she would not want for anything. 'Let's fix that, shall we?'

'So what do you do here, Sean Tate?' Gina ripped into a crab leg, sending shards of shell flying in all directions.

Sean picked the pieces of shell from his plate, raising his eyebrows at her before giving her a grin. 'I work with the Department of Foreign Affairs and Trade here in Bangkok. Vera and I were in Iran together on my first posting. Does she still have the hookahs and carpets?'

Gina laughed and rolled her eyes. 'Yees, and Jen hates them. She says their apartment is like Aladdin's cave.'

'Now there's a girl who knows how to shop.' Sean laughed, then nodded at Gina's empty plate. 'You know, I like a girl with a healthy appetite.'

'Like Rhett Butler.'

Sean nodded. 'In more than one way. Old-school charm isn't dead.'

Gina smiled, her eyes sparkling in a way which made him want to reach over and kiss her. *Take it slow. She's had a scare. Don't frighten her off*, he told himself. But every instinct screamed inside to grab hold of her and not let go.

'Scarlett is my heroine, you know.' She winked at him, eyes sparkling.

Sean swallowed. *If she keeps looking that way I'll be in trouble.* He laughed, hoping his face wasn't as transparent as Gina's, whose cheeks were now a hot pink as a blush crept over them. 'Explains a lot.'

Gina reached out and tapped him on the arm. 'Ha ha.' She sat back in her chair and folded her hands in her lap. 'What do you do for fun here?' she asked, her blush fading.

He took another sip of beer and looked straight into Gina's eyes. 'Practise rescuing damsels in distress. Especially dark-haired ones with blue eyes who have a thing for Rhett Butler.' He raised an eyebrow, hoping to make her blush once more.

It worked. 'Cheeky.' Gina leaned across to swipe him another blow but this time, tipped her drink over instead.

Sean grabbed his napkin and raced over to Gina, dropping the napkin over the flood of alcohol spreading towards Gina's lap. 'You are a handful.' He leant down and whispered in her ear, mouth watering at the smell of frangipani that radiated from her. He breathed her in, and his heart skipped.

Gina turned, looking up at him over her shoulder. 'Speaking metaphorically?' A playful smile spread across her lips.

Sean held his breath as their eyes locked. It had happened. He'd fallen in love. And there was nothing he could do to stop himself.

Chapter Seventeen

Gina wiped her clammy hands on her sarong as the taxi pulled into the airport. She'd lain awake most of the night, ruminating about Sean's warm smile and chivalrous manners. But every time her mind wandered to thoughts of them together, she pulled it back to reality. *He's being polite, that's all.* She surveyed her frizzy curls in her reflection on the window. There were plenty of lithe, elegant women everywhere in Bangkok, women who would not become intoxicated on one cocktail and disgrace themselves in restaurants. Demure, graceful women. Women he would no doubt prefer to her.

She paid the taxi driver and rolled her bag into the cool of the air-conditioned terminal, heart quickening as she entered the airport's sprawl. *In three hours you will be on the plane. Then you can forget Travis, and Sean.* She gripped the handle of her bag and turned to find the Air Niugini sign.

'Here, let me help with that.'

Gina smiled. *Surely it can't be.* Her heart skipped as she turned to see Sean smiling at her once again.

'Thanks for everything'. She clutched the gaudy prawn souvenir Sean had bought for her at the souvenir shop; prawns swimming amongst glittery seaweed and flashing, coloured lights. A cacophony of experiences, like this trip. It had more ups and downs than a cardiograph display, but every time her emotions or fears dipped into negative territory, Sean rescued her. Nevertheless, he wasn't *her* knight in shining armour. Gina's chin wobbled as she tried to hold back her tears.

'It's over, now. You're safe.' Sean pulled her to him, his arms locked around her back, and her heart slowed.

I feel safe. I feel . . . home. Gina closed her eyes and nestled into his shoulder, tears dripping on to Sean's shirt. *You've been wrong about men before,* she reminded herself. But her self-talk was no match for Sean's cologne, calling to her nostrils like a siren song. *He smells so good.* She nuzzled into his neck, inching closer and closer. *I wonder if he tastes as good as he smells?* Before she realised she'd done it, she had placed a gentle kiss on his cool skin.

In a deft movement, Sean's lips locked with hers, his tongue exploring her mouth with a passionate urgency that made her light-headed. His hands moved across her back, protective and hungry all at once. *It doesn't feel like goodbye.*

'Flight PX 345 to Port Moresby is now ready for boarding.'

But it was goodbye.

'Try and stay out of trouble in future.' He tapped her on the backside.

No 'I'll call you'. Nothing.

It was over. Whatever 'it' was.

'I'll try.' Gina kissed him and drew back, her eyes brimming with tears as she walked away.

Gina turned her face away from the plane window as an old woman took the seat beside her. She had wished to be alone and had initially turned her head out of politeness, but her new companion looked at her with eyes so full of kindness, and a glint of mischief, that she couldn't help giving her a genuine smile.

'It's never easy parting when you're in love.' She nodded at the window. 'He's a lovely lad.'

'Isn't he?' Gina brightened.

'Trudy Nelson.' The woman nodded at her.

'Gina Trent.'

'So how long have you two been an item, dear?'

'We're not. It was just a kiss.' Gina leaned back in her seat.

'Looked like more than a kiss from where I stood.' Mrs Nelson chuckled.

'Do you think?' Gina swivelled to face Mrs Nelson. 'Because it felt like more than just a kiss. But I don't know if I trust my judgment.'

Mrs Nelson's eyes narrowed. 'We'll need a drink for this one, I think.' She turned to the hostess now at her side. 'Two white wines please. Each.'

'The thing is, Mrs Nelson; I think I know where things are headed, but I'm always blindsided.' Gina sighed.

Mrs Nelson patted her hand. 'I was the same until I met my husband. I lived on a farm and was out to impress one of the shearers. I was wearing in my Sunday best, walking around the paddock, when the neighbour's dog got loose. He was a vicious thing and saw me and gave chase. I ran as best I could in my dress and shoes, breaking a heel and falling over near the fence line. I was expecting the dog to attack me but instead I heard it howl and a man yelling at it. I looked up at a handsome man with a stick in one hand, holding out the other to help me off the ground. He was Fred Dickens from the farm next door, the son of my neighbour. The last time I'd seen him he'd been a gangly looking teenager. My, how he'd changed.'

Mrs Nelson took a sip of her wine and Gina chuckled to herself. *A woman after my own heart.*

'For years I dated other men, and Fred and I became friends. But then my fiancé left. Just upped and disappeared without a word.' Her eyes gleamed. 'But that was when Fred showed me how he felt.'

'But Sean didn't ask for my number. I have to use my head.'

Mrs Nelson frowned. 'Has using your head worked for you so far?'

Gina's face reddened.

'Sometimes you need to trust what's in here.' Mrs Nelson touched her heart.

Gina looked at her tray. 'Mine leads me astray every time.' She gulped as she remembered her baby's white bonnet. If she was ever to have the chance of being a mother again, she had to use her head. Her heart would only mess things up.

And whatever her heart said about Sean, her head contradicted.

My Dream Man (Revised)

1. Dark hair.

2. Taller than me (logistics matter).

3. Wants a relationship and a family (rather than a fling, friends-with-benefits or variation thereof).

4. Isn't a cyclist or a triathlete (why are they all nuts? Besides, someone who is more worried about his calorie intake than me and who shaves his legs is too effeminate).

5. Has a job (failed business men trying to 'find themselves' need not apply. Do I look like an ATM?).

6. No Geminis – why do the ones I date always have a psycho personality as their part of their twin nature?

7. No criminal record (I'm thinking of you, Travis).

8. My age or older (Travis again . . .)

Chapter Eighteen

Will Lockwood gazed at the ring as the plane descended at Manchester Airport, before closing the box and slipping it into the pocket of his linen jacket.

The last six months apart from Naomi had been harder than he wanted to admit. They had met at university and it was a case of opposites colliding in a noisy tangle of limbs and sexual moans. Now, over a decade later, they had settled into a comfortable pattern. He didn't have to do anything, besides pay for her clothes, shoes and a professional wardrobe consultant. She devoted herself to looking after him. It was an easy coexistence.

He'd thought about getting engaged often during their separation, but the call from his mother, asking him to come home from Tokyo to see his father before he passed, was the sign he needed.

Naomi loved attention, so he'd decided on an airport proposal; it was public, to satisfy her, and immediate, to satisfy him.

The immigration queue, however, was not cooperating. The counter staff moved at a glacial pace, as if testing his patience. Will tapped his foot next to his Louis Vuitton suit bag. *Naomi will be furious*, he thought as he crept closer to the front of the line. He tried her phone again, but it went straight to voicemail. *Probably trying to park, heaven help the other cars*. He smiled as he ended the call, and rehearsed the words he'd say. Nothing outlandish, just a simple 'I love you, will you be my wife?' Will frowned as he looked at the queue in front of him. Couldn't they move any quicker? Didn't they know he had a proposal to make? He took in a deep breath. *Calm, Lockwood. Can't propose when you're angry.*

When he had progressed through the gate, he bobbed his head left and right, looking for Naomi's blonde locks. *Maybe she was stuck in traffic?* He stood, watching as other couples embraced, and tried Naomi's number once more.

Two hours later, Will wound his way through airport traffic in the back of a taxi. *After six months away she can't even pick me up from the airport on time.*

Then anger gave way to worry.

Naomi had been her usual effusive self when he called her from the airport in Tokyo. They had bantered about which puppy they would buy. Naomi wanted a Bichon Frisé; but he had grown up with black Labradors, and now he was settling with Naomi, it seemed right to continue the tradition in his own family. There was no hint of trouble. And no messages since then to say she'd had to deal with an emergency.

She didn't work, so she hadn't been called in for a work emergency, either.

He willed the taxi to drive faster, jaw clenching as the tyres swished through rain-moistened streets.

He couldn't do anything until he arrived home. Or until Naomi answered her phone.

Will's stomach flip-flopped for another twenty minutes, his calls to Naomi continuing to go through to voicemail. When they reached the house, a leaden heaviness filled his belly. The curtains were drawn, and the rubbish piled high.

He gave the driver a large tip before bounding out the door; not even waiting for his luggage. *She's been doing a clean out. She's collapsed inside. She's in the hospital.*

He put the key in the lock, heart in his mouth as his

mind ticked through various possibilities.

But as soon as he opened the front door, the dead houseplants confirmed his fears.

Naomi had left him.

In the bank the next day, Will checked his phone yet again. No new messages. He'd go round to Naomi's again after he banked this client's cheque. There had been no sign of her last night, and her parents in Spain weren't answering their phone. The police had been little help, telling him to come back the day after next, and hinting that he was somehow to blame for the situation. Meanwhile, he'd been replaying disastrous scenarios, finally deciding to put his energy to better use by working.

'Mr Lockwood, your account is overdrawn by £10,000.' The clerk's eyes darted from Will to the printout in her hand.

'I beg your pardon?'

'Your business partner withdrew a large amount yesterday.'

Will's mind raced.

As the clerk handed over the documents his jaw hardened. There was Naomi's signature. She was a signatory on the account, for emergencies only.

He groaned as he remembered. Naomi had mentioned something about a bill that had to be paid for the business. It hadn't made sense at the time, he had all bills handled by the accountant. He'd told her to email it through to the accounting firm.

Thought it had all been taken care of.

He shook his head. She'd taken care of it all right.

She had cleared out and cleared him out.

***

Will opened the bottle of Grange he had planned to open on their engagement. 'Cheers.' He flopped on to the sofa and flicked on the sound system. The chances of recovering the money were slim, but there was a principle to defend. Naomi would pay for the hole she'd left in his heart, and the humiliation she'd heaped him with.

Was she really interested in me? Or was it just the money? Thinking back, there were signs of their lack of compatibility, which he'd ignored in favour of lust.

And he'd paid the price. *From now on it's head first, then heart.*

He let his favourite Beatles track wash over him. 'Yesterday, all my troubles seemed so far away.' His voice broke on the last word. At least someone understood what he was experiencing, even if they were five dead musicians.

'Brrrrrring.' The sharp clang of the doorbell made him jump.

Will turned down the music and glared at the door. *Eleven p.m. on a school night. Who the hell is that?* He threw his scrunched up tie on to the sofa and padded to the door.

When he opened it, he was greeted by a grinning Naomi in a figure-hugging dress.

'Hi baby,' she purred, leaning in for a kiss. The smell of alcohol wafted up to him. *How could I have spent one day with this creature?*

Will put his hands out to stop her, bile rising in his throat. 'Bit late for that,' he sneered. 'Come on.' He nodded at the street. As tempted as he was to slam the door in her face, he couldn't leave her on the street when she was drunk. He wasn't a Neanderthal.

Naomi stepped back, brow furrowed. Still thought she could use sex to get what she wanted. Well, he was wiser than that now.

Will pulled the door to behind him and strode to the street to hail her a cab, Naomi's heels clipping along behind him.

'Baby don't be angry. I'm sorry. It was all a mistake.'

Will groaned and opened the door of the cab that had pulled up. 'Sod off. And pay me back my £10,000.'

Chapter Nineteen

When Sean's texts and emails waned, Gina turned to her hairdresser for some pampering.

What she was getting, though, was a lecture.

'These men on the Internet – no good,' Richard said with a flamboyant wave of the colouring brush. 'This Travis could have murdered you in your sleep. You lucky you back here with me, gorgeous.' Richard stirred her hair colour with vigour.

'Richard, I'm over it. The harder I try, the worse things get. So, I'm not going to make any more lists or plans.'

Richard stopped stirring and squinted at her in the mirror.

'You do nothing, huh? How long this last? I know you; you no sit still for two minutes.'

Gina squirmed under the cape, which had become steamy. She opened her mouth to protest, but Richard wagged his finger at her and continued colouring.

So much for pampering, Gina thought as she left the salon. She caught the familiar twang of Australian men chattering in the courtyard of the hotel. 'So are we going to the Gold Club tonight?' They laughed as they scraped their chairs back on the tiles.

Gina glared at them, her antipathy for men having grown stronger with each minute Sean didn't call. But it fell away when a tall, dark man amongst the party looked up at her and caught her eye.

Oh. My. Goodness.

Max Hampton. Dishy policeman and former piece of office eye-candy. She'd fantasised about Max when they'd worked together, but he was married. Still, one could admire. *What's he doing here, though?*

Max walked towards her; his million-dollar smile glinting in the sun. 'Gina. Fancy meeting you here.' He kissed her on the cheek and gestured for her to sit, his hand slipping on to her back as they walked towards a table. Gina stiffened. *He shouldn't be doing that. What would his wife think?* She frowned.

She let Max pull her chair out and held her handbag on her lap in front of her. *I'll just stay a minute, then say I have to go.*

Max leaned over the table. 'You look great.'

Gina blushed and looked at the ground to hide her frown. Max was definitely flirting with her, despite having a wife and children at home. Creep. 'Thanks.'

'So are you married? Do you have kids?' Max glanced at her hands.

Gina looked at the empty ring finger on her left and her face burned. 'No.'

'Neither am I.'

Gina whipped her head up.

'It happened eighteen months ago. The kids are with my ex and I'm here now with a consultancy firm.'

Gina's heart beat faster. Max single- and flirting with her.

A slow smile crept over her face, which Max answered with a brilliant one of his own- along with a raised eyebrow.

'So, now that we've got that cleared up, are you free for lunch?'

A week later, Gina dissected her lunch date with Jen. 'I used to drool over Max, and now he lands in my lap.' Gina shrugged her shoulders. 'Go figure.' She didn't add that she wished it was Sean landing in her lap.

He hadn't called. She'd been wrong-again. And it seemed she'd been wrong about Max, too.

'Hmm, so tell me more about this landing in laps. Sounds kinky. Ooh, wait until I light this cigarette.' Jen closed her eyes as she drew on the cigarette.

'Well, he picked me up and waited by the car, and opened the door for me. And we talked the whole time.' Gina sighed.

'So far it sounds like you're reeling off a shopping list. Why do I sense a but coming?'

Gina shook her head. 'He didn't offer to pay the bill at the end. I guess he was just wanted to talk about old times.' She shrugged. 'He seemed so keen though.'

Jen rolled her eyes. 'Maybe he is keen, and was sussing you out for a real date?' She flicked her ash into an ashtray with the red, yellow and black colours of the PNG flag. Jen had a quirky liking for kitch. 'Relax.'

Gina glanced out over the harbour's sparkling blue water.

'I know what you're doing. You're trying to kill this off because you want Sean.' Jen took a puff on her cigarette, one eye closed, another gimlet eye trained on Gina.

'No I'm not.' Gina's cheeks flushed.

'Are too. But you don't understand male psychology. You're acting taken, when you're not. And I bet Sean's picking up the vibes.'

Gina frowned. 'Rubbish.' But her voice was tentative. What if Jen was right? What if she was scaring Sean away on some metaphysical level?

'Look, it's simple. Use Max to make Sean jealous and have a bit of fun, and stop worrying so much about who might be "the one".' Jen grinned. 'Just relax.'

Gina laughed. 'Me, relax?' That was as simple as asking the sun to stop shining. What Jen said made sense, though. Maybe she was being too uptight. But using Max to signal some universal message to Sean didn't seem right. She sighed. It was all getting too complicated. 'What does it matter? Max won't call anyway.'

Jen raised an eyebrow at her. 'You don't know that. Go with the flow, remember?' She stubbed out her cigarette and pulled another out of its bright blue box. 'Hey, maybe you should channel your inner control freak into S&M . . .'

Gina's jaw fell open. 'Jen!' Her phone beeped, and their eyes swivelled towards its screen, where the name Max flashed beside the answer button. *Oh no. Now what do I do?*

Jen grabbed the phone. 'Ha! Told you! Now, say yes.'

Sean took a deep breath and stared at Gina's Skype photo, the air conditioner doing little to stem the perspiration pooling on his back. There was no point pretending he could control his feelings for Gina anymore. He was now so addlepated that he was forgetting things; even turning up for work this morning wearing two different coloured shoes.

Something Gina would do.

I'll suggest we meet up again. I'll fly her up here. See how things go. She isn't Leigh.

He pressed the call button, heart thumping in his chest. Would she be happy to hear from him? He hadn't wanted to consider that scenario, but now, the beeping computer made him regret his haste.

I should have emailed first, made a time to talk with her. Just in case she's with someone.

He swallowed, and moved the mouse over the 'end call' button. He still had time. He lowered his finger on to the mouse, then Gina's face appeared on the webcam; a tight smile on her lips.

His stomach sank. Too late now; not only to end the call, but, he sensed, to say what he planned to say to Gina.

'Hi. I hope I didn't call at a bad time?' It had to be the

worst opening line in history. Sean attempted a smile, while groaning inwardly.

Gina bit the corner of her lip; an almost imperceptible movement, but one that told him more than her words could. 'No, not at all.' She waved her hand away, but wouldn't look into the webcam.

Sean's stomach clenched. There was no going back now, he couldn't end the call all of a sudden. The only way was through.

He cleared his throat and willed his voice to stay steady. 'Fine. You?'

Sean nodded. 'Good. Busy with work.' He gazed into the camera. 'You must be out a lot on dates.' He attempted a smile.

Gina blushed. He was right.

'Who is he?'

Gina sighed. 'Just someone from work. It's nothing.' She shrugged.

Sean nodded. 'You don't know that yet.'

Gina's head whipped up and her jaw clenched.

I said the wrong thing. I was trying to be encouraging. Couldn't even get that right.

'Yeah. I guess I don't.'

This is painful. I shouldn't have called. Sean watched as Gina's eyes glanced downwards. If he didn't end the call now, it would become even more awkward. He knocked his knuckles beneath the desk. 'Ah, I can hear someone at the door. Sorry, I'd better go.'

Gina nodded.

'Take care of yourself.' Sean tried to swallow, but his throat was dry.

'You too.' Gina pursed her lips, then the screen went blank.

Sean leaned back into his chair and groaned. He was too late.

My Dream Man: Max?

1. Dark hair – Check, Max has gorgeous hair.

2. Taller than me – Check.

3. Wants a relationship and a family (rather than a fling, friends-with-benefits or variation of) – Hmm, to be determined . . .

4. Isn't a cyclist or a triathlete – Check.

5. Has a job – Check.

6. No Geminis – Check.

7. No criminal record – Check.

8. My age or older – Check.

Chapter Twenty

For all her concerns about Max's intentions, he had proven to be an ardent suitor. He sent her amorous text messages every morning, and visited her at work just to see how her day was.

So far, he was perfect.

Gina smiled to herself as the light evening breeze caressed her bare arms. Max had surprised her with a mysterious dinner invitation, along with the delivery of a dress and jewellery for the occasion.

It was what men did in movies. And now it was happening to her.

Finally, something was going right.

Gina touched the gold pendant at her neck: a bird of paradise. Genuine gold, judging by its heaviness. Worth at least two thousand kina, she guessed. No one had spent that much money on her before. Not even Alex. Or . . . Sean. She bit her lip as a pang of guilt made her chest twinge. He'd looked so deflated when she'd told him she was dating. Why hadn't he called earlier?

It's his own fault, she reminded herself. *He had his chance.*

'You look amazing.' Max touched her arm as they crossed the driveway, and she let her free hand drop from the pendant. 'In fact . . .' he stopped and pulled her in for a kiss, not a hint of concern that they might be run over at any moment.

I should tell him to wait, Gina thought, the protest melting away as Max's lips touched hers. *But then why shouldn't I enjoy being adored for once?* Gina closed her eyes, losing herself in his eager kiss.

The guards on the car park gate sniggered in the background, then a whistle rang out.

Not that Max cared. His hands were now caressing her backside.

'Max, not here,' Gina whispered as he started kissing her neck. Adoration was one thing, but this was getting out of control. The last thing she needed was someone reporting her to her Canberra.

He clenched her backside, making her yelp. 'Max,' Gina hissed, pulling his hand away.

Then a horn tooted.

Where did that car come from? Gina glanced to her right, hoping the driver wasn't someone she worked with.

Her eyes widened as she looked at Alex's frowning face.

'Come on.' Gina looked away and ran a hand through her hair, hoping she didn't look as ravished as she felt.

'Get your hands off her.' Alex stalked towards them, car door left open as the car idled.

Gina's heart raced. She'd never seen Alex angry before, and the look he was giving Max now was unmistakably malevolent.

Max moved Gina behind him as Alex reached them. They stood, puffing at each other like two old bulls.

The guards weren't laughing now. From the corner of her eye she could see them, standing. Watching.

She had to do something.

Gina moved out from behind Max. She had to make some distance between the two of them. '*You* don't get to tell me what to do anymore.'

Alex's chest heaved as he looked at her. 'Gina, you don't understand who this bastard really is.' He jabbed a finger in the air in Max's direction.

Gina gave an exasperated laugh. Alex had given her up,

and now she was happy with someone else, he decided to play the protective man? Well he'd had his chance, too. 'You're pathetic. You don't want me, but you don't want anyone else to have me, either.'

Alex shook his head. 'No, it's not like that.' He reached his hands out to place them on her shoulders, but she stepped aside.

'Don't you touch me,' she sneered, glaring at him. She was tempted to reach out and slap him, but the guards were now moving towards them.

Alex followed her gaze, then looked back at her, his eyes narrowed. 'Gina, I *need* to talk to you.' His neck cords strained.

Her stomach tightened. Something about that look told he she should be worried; but she was too angry to heed it. She had come so far, and now Alex wanted to ruin it.

He didn't have that right.

Gina lifted her chin. 'Well, I'm done talking to you.'

Alex's shook his head and she turned and stalked past Max towards the restaurant. She didn't want everyone seeing her crying.

Max's footsteps sounded behind her, and in a moment, his hand was on the small of her back. 'You okay?'

Gina nodded. 'I'm fine.' She looked up at Max, whose eyes were scanning her upturned face.

'You sure?'

Gina tried not to sigh. No, she wasn't sure. One minute she was enjoying a Hollywood moment, the next, Alex ruined it. And she could not shake the sense that worse was to come. She took a deep breath, hoping to dispel the emotional cloud that now hung over her.

'Come on, we won't let him ruin our night.' Max put his arm around her shoulder, and Gina snuggled into it, willing her mood to improve.

Make me feel safe, she thought, *the way Sean did.*

Max squeezed her to him, as if sensing her need for reassurance. 'Don't worry about him, he's just jealous.'

Gina gave a small nod, waiting for that sense of calm she'd experienced with Sean. In his arms she'd known all would be well, with him by her side.

Now, all she felt was a rising lump of tears clogging in her throat.

It was happening again. It was all going wrong.

And Sean wasn't there to fix it.

After a sleepless night, Gina nursed her third mug of coffee, eyes swimming as she stared at the rows of budget figures on the spreadsheet before her. She'd thought the task would give her refuge from her whirling thoughts, and the doubts which had only grown during the dark hours of the night. Doubts about Max; but doubts too, about herself.

She was more concerned about preserving her idealised romance with Max than hearing what Alex had to say. But was she only prolonging the inevitable in doing so?

It wasn't the action of a strong, assured woman; the woman she'd thought she had become.

The sound of a heavy step on the veranda made her look up.

'Excuse me, where is Gina working, please?'

Gina caught her breath. *Alex.*

She glanced at the open curtains at her window. She couldn't pretend she was out, everyone at the office knew she was in.

She took in a deep, deliberate breath. It was a sign. Whatever he had to say, she needed to hear it.

Gina pushed the coffee cup away and reached for her breath mints. Might help wake her up.

Her teeth cracked into the sharp peppermint lolly, and she tried to ignore her now thudding heart.

Whatever Alex had to say, she would cope. She hoped.

She fixed her mouth into a hard line, pretending to read a document as Alex's footsteps neared, and a knock came at the door.

She stood, and walked to the door, balling her hands into fists by her side. *I've been hurt before and survived. I can do this.*

With a final gulp, she opened the door, giving Alex a cold glare.

'We need to talk.'

Gina gave a sharp nod, and stepped back to allow him to pass. The whole department would know about her male visitor by the end of the day, and if she argued with Alex at the door, they'd only invent even more elaborate gossip. Rumours grew like rampant tropical vines in this workplace.

'Take a seat.'

Gina shut the door and headed to the huddle of plastic chairs around the grey melamine table in the centre of her office. Only the blue and green basket in the centre, holding an assortment of pencils and other writing implements, hinted of the tropics. Max had bought it for her on their last trip to the markets.

She looked away from it, fixing her eyes instead on Alex.

His eyes were shadowed with dark circles, and new lines had formed on the sides of his eyes. He looked older than she remembered, and had an air of fragility he'd not shown before, not even when he'd been tender with her. Alex was always in control, even when he was being vulnerable.

He folded his hands and leant on the table. 'I don't want to see you get hurt.' He looked down at his hands. 'But you need to know that Max is still married.'

He looked up at her, eyes soft with concern.

'What?' Gina mumbled, her heart thudding. *He can't be. It isn't true.* She shook her head 'He said he was divorced . . .'

Alex sighed. 'Well, he's not. And, it gets worse, I'm sorry.' He cleared his throat. 'He's seeing other women here, besides you.'

Gina's mouth fell open.

'That's what I was trying to tell you last night.'

Gina exhaled as a wave of nausea rose up from her stomach, and Alex moved his hand towards her.

She stiffened. Alex Turner was the last person she wanted comforting her. She drew herself up in her seat, cheeks burning. She couldn't let him see he'd hurt her. 'And why should I believe a word you say?'

Alex met her gaze. 'Because I still care about you.'

Gina searched his eyes. He wasn't lying about that, she didn't think. But it was too little, too late.

She shook her head. 'Care about me? You have a funny way of showing it.' She sighed. 'You've ignored me for months, and now, when I finally pick up the pieces, you come back to mess me around again.'

'But I'm trying to protect you.'

Gina stood, raising her chin in the air. She knew Alex was right, but of all the people to deliver her this humiliation, why did it have to be the man who'd thrown her on to the single pile once more? 'I think you should go now.'

Alex stood. 'Look, if you need anything . . .'

Gina gave a low laugh. 'If I need anything, I won't ask you, so don't worry.' Her voice oozed sarcasm, and a level of enmity that surprised even her.

Alex nodded. 'Fair enough. But if you change your mind.'

'I won't.'

He strode to the door, looking over his shoulder, mouth

open to speak; but Gina slammed the door and leant against it, willing the sobs rising up from deep inside her belly not to escape.

Max wouldn't lie to her – would he?

She darted to her desk, grabbed her phone and dialled Max's number.

What did she really know about him? She hadn't seen him for ten years.

She needed to hear his voice, and then she'd know.

'Hey babe, was just thinking about you.' Max purred the words; words she would have viewed as adoring, but now, they seemed fake.

Gina cleared her throat. There was only one way to find out. 'Are you still married?'

Silence.

'Technically yes, but . . .'

Gina let out a sob, before pressing the button to end the call.

Travis, now Max – it's like being trapped in a Bridget Jones style version of Alice in Wonderland. Her breathing slowed in the silence. *If I have a plan, it goes wrong. If I don't have a plan, it goes wrong.* She stood up and shut her curtains, before letting her silent tears fall.

Gina reached for the chocolate bar sitting half-eaten on the table at breakfast the next day, the remnants of midnight snacking. Max hadn't called back, and Alex had sent her a text message asking if she was okay. She'd ignored it.

Of course she wasn't okay. But she wasn't admitting that to him.

Slumping into a chair, she caught sight of a book on her shelf: *From Commitment-Phobe to Commitment-Mad.* Alli had given it to her when she and Alex first broke up, and she'd let it gather dust until now. Flicking through the pages, her thumb caught on a page titled *The Narcissist*.

Fifteen minutes later, she laid the book on her lap.

Alex met every one of the criteria. So did Max, and Travis.

If only I'd read this book before, she thought, biting her lip. *But then, would I have paid any attention if I had?*

Probably not.

She frowned. She wouldn't have recognised the patterns; patterns that were now clear to her.

She pulled a nearby writing pad on to her lap, and grabbed a pen, jotting down the common characteristics of the men she'd dated.

How different would her life have been if she'd had this list years ago?

She nodded. That was it. She didn't have the list, but she could share it with other women, and stop them making the same mistakes.

The List was born.

Ten minutes later, *The List* had a Facebook site.

Thirty minutes later it had one hundred likes.

The next day it had five hundred.

The List had gone viral.

Chapter Twenty One

A week later in Manchester, Will strode into his local pub with as much confidence as he could muster. The familiar smell of musty carpet rose up to greet him, like an old friend.

He could use a friend right now, real or imagined, on his first Internet date.

The nerves had passed, and now, like the grumpy old man he feared he was, he was peeved. Internet dating, for goodness sake. It was the domain of men like his colleague Seamus, who lacked the ability to talk to women. He, however, had always drawn women to him.

But the dating world had changed since he'd last been single.

He shook his head as he sat in the back corner booth he and Tayah had agreed on.

Still, she'd seemed normal compared to the other women he'd encountered. One woman had sent him half-naked pictures after they'd exchanged one email. Another had bombarded him with emails for two consecutive days while he'd been on a business trip; ending with angry rants about male patriarchy and his lack of humanity. And all he'd done was be too busy to respond to her immediately.

He glanced at the bar with a dry mouth. It was polite to wait until he ordered a drink, but right now, he'd like to sod being a gentleman.

Will looked at his watch. Seven p.m. If she wasn't here in ten minutes, he'd leave. Hamish and Phoebe were on standby for a post-date drink, and, if he was lucky, some of Phoebe's left-over lasagne.

A tall, blonde woman entered the pub, giving a tentative glance around the room.

She looked exactly like her photo. Phew. Poor Seamus's last date looked nothing like her photo.

He breathed out and broke into a smile, standing to greet her.

Maybe this will turn out all right after all.

It had taken Will ten minutes of conversation with Tayah to realise he needed to escape, and fast. 'So when I'm preparing for a shoot I only drink juices. It costs me a fortune.' Tayah laughed. Will restrained the temptation to groan. If he heard any more about the intricacies of spray tanning and fake nails he'd say something regretful.

'What do you do on weekends?' he asked, hoping to change the subject.

'Stay in bed.'

Will jerked as a warm hand landed on his thigh under the table, inching its way upwards.

Tayah raised her eyebrows and giggled, until he clamped his hand over hers.

He didn't need to say anything, the look he gave her was enough. She withdrew her hand with a nonchalant shrug.

'Umm, early start for me tomorrow I'm afraid. Lovely to meet you though.' He stood, barely giving Tayah a nod before striding from the pub.

It wasn't gentlemanly. He should have seen her safe to a cab. Will glanced backwards, but Tayah was sauntering towards the young, grinning barman.

He laughed. Well, at least someone might go home happy tonight.

Will sighed and pushed against the pub door, taking in a gulp of the crisp night air.

It will happen, just give it time, he reminded himself as he headed to the car. He'd always been lucky, and he'd be lucky in love, too – eventually.

Gina heaved her suitcase on to the conveyor belt at Brisbane Airport's check-in counter. Her new assistant, Kara, had helped her purchase a suite of mix and match outfits befitting her status as an online entrepreneur. She now looked like a business-woman, even if she didn't quite believe it herself.

She sat down in the airline lounge seat with a bundle of magazines and a gin and tonic, closing her eyes when she'd finished the drink. Often, when she went to sleep, she wondered whether she would open her eyes to her old life; a life of accepting less than she deserved.

She'd done so with all the men she'd dated in a way, but she was getting stronger. She did confront Max, after all; and she hadn't chased Alex, either.

Nor had she chased Sean.

She frowned. She'd dreamed about Sean last night, of him holding her in his arms and kissing her on a boat. But there was a little girl with her, a girl she'd known was her daughter.

Wishful thinking, that's what it was. She had no one else in her life, and she was projecting all her future desires on to Sean, just because he hadn't disappointed her as badly as the others.

But that didn't mean he wouldn't.

So many times she'd been tempted to call him, but stopped herself. He'd made it clear he didn't want to speak to her. She had to find her own strength now.

A coughing at her side made her open one eye.

It wasn't.

She opened another.

Oh no. It was.

Gina sat up, running her hands through her hair. Of all

the times to return to her life, Sean Tate chose the moment she was napping in an airline lounge.

Well, he might have her at a disadvantage, but she wasn't going to show it.

He sat down opposite her. 'Did you enjoy your nana nap?'

Gina lifted her chin. 'I wasn't sleeping.'

'No, not at all.' His smile widened into a grin and he nodded at the empty glass on the table.

Her cheeks flushed. Of course he had to labour the point that she'd had a drink. Fine, she'd just make a quip about his moodiness the last time they spoke.

Gina opened her mouth to deliver her retort when Sean winked at her.

What?

Gina's cheeks warmed, and she dropped her eyes to the table. He'd been so tetchy when she'd mentioned Max in their last call, yet now he was flirting with her. Not that she minded.

'You look fantastic. Even if you *are* tipsy.'

Gina raised her eyes to his, her gaze cloudy. Flirting was difficult enough while sober, but after a gin and tonic, she couldn't be sure her words would come out as she intended. She searched for a suitable response.

'I bet you say that to all the girls.' Her voice had the husky tone of a coquette, and Sean's eyes twinkled.

Great. Now I'm flirting back, when I should be rousing on him.

'No, I don't actually.' He raised an eyebrow, and leaned back into his chair.

Gina caught her breath as their eyes locked, earlier thoughts of angry repartee forgotten.

If they were alone, she'd be tempted to lean over and kiss him. Her eyes zeroed in again on the gentle curves of his lips. *Control yourself, Gina.*

She settled back into her chair and raised an eyebrow in

return. Sean was clearing the fogginess from her system quicker than coffee ever could. 'You've changed your tune.' There. Let him flirt his way out of that.

Sean's smile faded. 'Yeah. Sorry about that. And sorry about Max.'

She had no chance of staying angry with him, she knew, especially when he looked at her with those dancing hazel eyes.

Gina waved her hand. 'Oh, I suppose I can forgive you.'

His smile returned, as did the sparkle in his eye. 'Good. Are you free tomorrow? I need to buy some souvenirs at the market. I could use your help.'

Gina laughed, marvelling at how easily they slipped back into their easy banter. 'Oh, so you only want me for my shopping skills, do you?'

Their eyes locked.

Gina's every muscle vibrated with expectation. He wasn't looking away. He was smiling, and now he was laughing.

Was this really happening? Was he really here, looking at her with such desire that she wanted to launch herself over the table at him?

He was, and now he was leaning forward, beckoning her to lean towards him; his cologne making her mouth water. 'Shopping is just a warm up,' he whispered, his breath soft and warm on her ear.

Gina swallowed, then shivered as Sean brushed the backs of his fingers over her exposed upper arm. He'd hurt her, yet here he was, luring her towards him. And she wasn't interested in stopping him.

You should be smarter, she told herself. *Find your own strength, remember?*

And then, as if in slow motion, she was lifting her face to his, and their lips were touching.

Being strong or smart didn't matter anymore.

All that did matter was Sean.

Chapter Twenty Two

The next morning, Gina stifled a yawn as she waited outside Sean's hotel, a languorous smile parting her lips.

Tonight she planned to be awake, but for a very different reason, she thought as Sean strode to the car. *Except he wants to go shopping, when I'd rather be . . .* Her mouth filled with saliva as she watched Sean open the door; every second drawing her closer to his presence.

'Hi.'

Gina swallowed as he slid into his seat. If she was more of a coquette she'd have some seductive line ready, but a simple 'Hi' was all she could manage.

Sean leaned over and placed a soft kiss on her lips, pulling away with a mischievous smile. 'Not too much of that, though, or we'll never get to the markets.'

Gina raised an eyebrow; his flirtiness fuelling her own. 'Hurry up then, the sooner we go the sooner we come back.'

Sean laughed and pulled on his seatbelt. 'Anticipation is half the fun.'

Gina smiled and shook her head. 'If you say so.' With a sigh, she switched the radio on and eased the car on to the road. No time to mull over what she'd rather be doing now, her eyes scanned both sides of the road, as she'd been taught to do in her safety briefing. Nothing except the usual milling of humanity, and no suspicious groups of people or sounds of shouting; the usual signs of trouble. She nodded as Sean talked.

'Can you believe it? Two women going to Mt Hagen, on their own – no security, nothing.' Sean shook his head.

'They wouldn't listen to me, either.'

'Hmmh, well you did all you could.' The blueness of Ela Beach glittered to her right and she turned towards Koki, her muscles tensing as neared the suburb. One of the worst places for carjackings; but Saturday mornings were usually safe. It was the quickest way to the markets, and the sooner she got there, the sooner she could be back at Sean's hotel.

She bit her lip to hide her smile as Sean continued with his diatribe; slowing as she came towards the pedestrian crossing. A typical Saturday morning parade of children, mothers and stall holders carrying their goods passed, and Gina tapped her fingers on the steering wheel.

Then the crowd thinned.

There was nothing obviously wrong with the men who started to cross, they carried long bundles of sticks, probably to sell. But the first one glanced behind at the other, and the hairs on Gina's arms stood on end.

Gina's eye caught the glint of metal, and in an instant the sticks had dropped, and the men were aiming guns at the windscreen.

Her body went rigid with fear and she sat, staring ahead, wondering whether the bullets would hurt when they pierced through her skin. She'd trained for a carjacking, but simulating one and having one happen in real life were vastly different experiences.

'Reverse. Quick.' Gina jumped, and jerked the gear stick back, steering the car back with increasing speed. She couldn't risk crashing the car, they'd be even more vulnerable then.

'Keep going!'

Gina was about to press the accelerator to the floor, when cars appeared on the road behind her, unaware of the danger they were heading towards.

'Shit!'

She slammed the brake and glanced back to the crossing. She could either risk hurting innocent people behind her, or try and get past the gunmen.

It was madness, she knew, driving towards armed men, but her muscles now vibrated with rage. If anyone thought they could push her around, they were mistaken.

She pushed the gear stick into drive and sped past towards the crossing, bullets peppering the windscreen only to bounce off the protective film.

'Fuck!'

Sean jumped in the seat beside her, turning to look behind them as more shots rang out. 'Just drive, Gina. Keep going.'

Her heart skipped in her chest as she zigzagged up Koki Hill's winding turns, her mind only focusing on the next curve and avoiding cars. But when the house with the coffin by the gate came into view, a lump rose in her throat.

If things had been different . . .

Tears prodded at the corner of her eyes.

'The Defence base is coming up, pull in there.'

Gina nodded, taking a deep breath. She had to get them to a safe place before she gave into her tears.

'You're doing great.' Sean reached out and put his hand on her shoulder. 'Not long now, just keep going.'

Gina turned into the road for the Defence base, coming to a stop at the guard hut. Her body shook, and Sean took his hand from her shoulder, before moving the gear stick into park.

'It's okay, you're safe now.' He pulled her towards him, rubbing his hands over her back.

She tried to nod, but her thoughts returned to the guns, and images of Sean sitting beside her, bloodied and unresponsive.

It could so easily have turned out that way.

She broke into a sob.

'Shhh.' Sean tightened his arms around her. 'You're all right. You're all right.' But she still shook, unable to dispel the other disastrous endings she could have faced. She'd read about stories of violent crime so much that she'd become immune to their true horror, until now, when the violence was happening to her.

She blinked, her lashes heavy with tears. *You're safe, you made it,* she told herself. But even in Sean's arms, she couldn't quite believe it.

Chapter Twenty Three

'I'm fine,' Gina protested, sitting on to Jen's guest bed with a thump. It had been two days since the carjacking, but Jen had refused to let her return home.

'No, you're not.' Jen held out two sleeping tablets the doctor had left her that afternoon. 'You need to sleep.'

Sean walked in and exchanged a glance with Jen. 'You try.' Jen held the tablets out to Sean, who turned up his palm to catch them.

She's like a mother bear, Gina thought as Jen closed the door behind her.

'She's so bossy.' Gina sighed. While it was nice to have someone cooking for her and keeping her company, she hadn't had a moment alone, except to go to the toilet. And even then, Jen knocked at the door if she took too long.

'Well, she needs to be. You're very stubborn,' Sean replied, tapping her nose with his forefinger. 'Take them. For me?' he asked, holding the tablets out to her. 'You can't go another night without a good rest.'

His eyes searched hers; now rimmed with dark circles. Sean hadn't gone to work since the carjacking, staying up with her for as long as he could.

Sleeping tablets. She pursed her lips. Medication wasn't her first choice, she preferred reading. Not that her bleary eyes could make out the words too well. It was the only time she'd wished someone would read the book to her – but she wasn't about to ask.

Sleep *would* be nice. And she couldn't continue worrying everyone.

'Okay.' She nodded, taking the pills and swallowing them with the glass of water Sean handed her.

Sean put the glass on to the bedside table 'Why don't I tell you a story? Lull you to sleep with my dulcet tones?' He grinned at her.

Gina's jaw fell open. He knew what she needed, and she hadn't said a word.

She was tempted to kiss him, but she knew if she did, she would start crying, and might not stop. When he touched her arm, or hugged her, the tears poked at her eyes, and she would swallow hard, forcing them back.

Sean peered at her. 'No?' He gave a theatrical shrug. 'I got rave reviews for my year five play, you know.' He cocked an eyebrow at her.

Gina laughed, and for a moment, the memories and fears stilled. 'Okay, you've sold me.'

'I knew that would clinch it.' He propped pillows up against the wall. 'Scoot up here next to me then, while I tell you a tale that will bore you to sleep.'

Gina bit her lip as she nestled next to Sean's comforting warmth. 'Well. It all started when we had to order my new official passport. The way it works usually, is that . . .'

Her body, which was tight in places she didn't even realise she could tighten; eased in his presence. She sighed as her breath worked its way into the muscles she'd clenched. Who knew that tight muscles could be so painful? But it could have been worse . . .

A tear slid down her cheek, and she moved to wipe it away. *Not now. Don't cry in front of him,* she thought, moving to wipe her other cheek, when Sean's finger brushed her skin.

She kept her eyes closed, not wanting to break the spell when Sean took her hand in his, and rubbed his thumb over hers. His voice, almost a whisper now, continued. Sexy, comforting, and nurturing, all at once.

I love you.

It bubbled up, as natural as breathing. Three little

words that meant so much, and which she'd been too scared to contemplate before.

She could think it. No harm in that.

Gina smiled and closed her eyes, letting Sean's voice drift over her as the delicious blackness of sleep enveloped her.

Perhaps it was the tablets, or perhaps she was delirious with exhaustion, but just before she succumbed to sleep, she thought she heard Sean say 'I love you', too.

The next morning, Sean padded out to join Vera on the balcony while she smoked her first cigarette. He stretched his arm, which had gone numb where Gina had lain during the night.

He smiled as he thought of her placid, sleeping face. He'd fallen asleep himself, eventually, after watching her most of the night; trying to assuage his guilt.

They stared at the cars coming and going from the port, saying nothing.

Vera patted him on the back. 'I am glad she was with you, mate. She likes to make out she's strong, but it's tough for a woman up here.'

Sean nodded, but couldn't reply. Yesterday a woman had been carjacked, and the thugs had raped her before leaving her in a settlement.

What if the attackers had stopped them, and taken Gina?

Sean clenched his jaw. He'd hesitated to let Gina know how he felt, and he couldn't tell her now. She needed someone now who was by her side every day. Something he couldn't offer.

He sighed. There was nothing to lose, though, by staying on and protecting her, as far as he could. No acting on his feelings.

Could he stop himself? He gritted his teeth.

It didn't matter. He didn't have a choice.

Gina needed him.

Sean cleared his throat. 'I'll be staying on for a few weeks, it seems.'

Vera turned to him, one eyebrow raised. 'Oh, right.'

'Work couldn't find anyone to replace me. Got a message this morning.' He looked away and pretended to inspect a bunch of dogs rooting through rubbish by the road below.

'I see.'

Sean clenched his jaw. Vera was no fool, she knew exactly what he was doing.

'Good decision,' she said, patting him on the back once more.

I hope so, he thought.

Chapter Twenty Four

Gina parked the car in the space the security guard pointed her to, in front of the restaurant's white Besser block wall. She'd thought about cancelling her monthly Yum Cha with Jen to spend more time with Sean; but the lure of her favourite custard tart dessert, and the maddening sexual tension between them had helped her make up her mind.

He'd not once tried to sleep with her. Not a hint.

She must have dreamed the 'I love you,' then.

Gina pursed her lips. There was being a gentleman, and there was being disinterested. Sean clearly fell into the latter category.

I can actually see myself with this guy, she thought. *He gives me something, instead of taking from me, like the others. But he doesn't want to stay, and there's nothing I can do.* With a resigned sigh, she eased herself out of the driver's seat; her pursed lips easing into a small smile as the warm sun caressed her skin. What would it be like for Sean to sweep his fingers across her skin, making it tingle like the sun's rays now did?

No point in dreaming about it, anymore.

'Has he said anything about keeping in contact when he leaves?' asked Jen as she divided out the turnip cakes.

'No. Probably doesn't want to keep in contact.' She jabbed her turnip cake with her chopstick.

'The turnip cake didn't deserve that.' Jen laughed. 'You are in sore need of a bit of – you know.'

Gina turned up her nose. 'But he doesn't want to.'

Jen crinkled her forehead. 'He's a man, of course he wants to.'

'Well, not this one.' Gina gave the turnip cake another

jab. 'And I don't blame him. He probably thinks I'm too needy.'

Jen rolled her eyes. 'Then he wouldn't have stayed, would he?'

Gina shrugged. 'He's a nice guy. He's not doing anything for me he wouldn't do for you, or Vera, or anyone else.'

Jen shook her head. 'Rubbish.'

Gina lifted her chin. 'I'm not getting ahead of myself for once. This time, I'm taking heed of the signs rather than ignoring them.'

Jen gave an exasperated sigh. 'It's obvious to anyone that he's mad about you.'

Gina glared at Jen, nostrils flaring. There was no point arguing with Jen, she was always right in her own mind; but she wasn't going to be told she was wrong about Sean. She'd ignored her head before and paid the price. And she was the one who had to deal with the consequences, not Jen or anyone else who offered their opinion on her love life. 'Well it's not obvious to me. End of story.'

'There we are, milady.' Sean gave a theatrical bow and placed an ice bucket and a bottle of champagne in front of Gina, clinking two glasses from behind his back on to the table with a swish. Things had been so tense between them that he'd decided to tell her about his move to Afghanistan in public. Safety in numbers.

Yes it was unfair. Gina hated showing her feelings in front of others. But if he told her the news at home, and she became upset, he'd have to comfort her, and one thing would lead to another, and he'd only hurt her more.

Sometimes, though, doing the right thing didn't feel right.

He could have turned the request down, but he'd hankered for this posting for years. Of course it would come, though, at a time when he wanted to stay where he was.

The Universe had a funny idea of timing, that was certain.

Gina looked at him, eyes narrowed slightly. 'Thanks.' Her icy tone suggested she was anything but grateful.

He poured champagne into her glass, avoiding her eyes. These past weeks he'd almost relented and told her how he felt. Thailand was only a plane ride away; they could make it work if he was there.

But Afghanistan was half a world away. Communication was intermittent, and the hours long. If they'd been dating a while, it might be different, but starting a new relationship under such conditions, when Gina was fragile already, would be a sure disaster.

She'd worry, they'd fight, and then they'd lose everything. He'd seen it before.

If they maintained a friendship though, they *could* be more than friends – one day.

Sean finished pouring, looking up now to see Gina looking at him with wide, sad eyes.

'It's the best they have. Thought you deserved it, after all you've been through.'

Their fingertips touched as he handed her the glass, and he swallowed. Lucky they were in public, or he'd be doing more than looking at her right now. He followed the gentle curve of Gina's cheek, tempted to reach out and stroke the soft, creamy skin of Gina's cheeks. Tempted to kiss her and tell her he loved her again. But he couldn't do it to her, or himself.

Sean looked down at the table to avoid her gaze.

He had to be strong for both of them, no matter how much Gina might hate him for it.

Chapter Twenty Five

Gina swirled the remnants of her coffee around in the cup, wrinkling her nose in distaste. Sean had been gone for an agonising month; his contact had become so intermittent she often wondered if she had dreamed their time together.

Gina wriggled as her clothes stuck to her skin. It was only 10 a.m., and Jen's fan whirred from the corner of the balcony, doing little to ease the oppressive heaviness of the humid tropical air, which was almost as heavy as her mood.

Her thoughts had turned back to the pink polka dotted box with alarming regularity in the weeks since Sean had gone. If she'd allowed her feelings to guide her, she would have been repeating the past. *At least this time I used my head rather than my heart,* she reminded herself.

When alone, she was sure she'd been right not to tell Sean how she truly felt about him. But with every passing day, she doubted her choice – and Jen was not helping matters.

'You should have just made a move on him.' Jen flicked her cigarette into the ashtray. 'At least then you'd have happy memories.'

'I *do* have happy memories.' Gina sat upright in her chair.

'Not the sort *I* mean, though.' Jen blew the cigarette smoke out of the side of her mouth. 'Call him. Tell him what you want.'

Gina shook her head.

'Oh for heaven's sake. You're a catch. Why can't you see

what I see? What Sean sees?'

Gina's chin wobbled. 'Because it's not true.' Gina gritted her teeth in an attempt to stop her tears. 'I'm a bad person. And if Sean knew what I was really like, he'd . . .'

Jen frowned and leaned forward. 'Bad? You're one of the nicest people I know.'

Gina shook her head, tears now spilling down her cheeks. 'No I'm not. I didn't want my first baby,' Gina burst out, 'and the baby died.' Her chest heaved. 'It was my fault she died.'

Jen's jaw fell open. 'What?'

Gina closed her eyes and took a deep breath. She'd tried, and failed, to deal with her guilt alone; and if she kept on the path she was on, she'd never keep the promise she'd made to the baby she lost. She needed help, and Jen was determined enough for both of them.

Gina opened her eyes, and Jen gave her an encouraging nod. 'My boyfriend at the time had always said he didn't want kids, and I had no job. He left me, then I found out I was pregnant.' Gina looked down at her hands. 'I thought about getting rid of it.' Gina raised her eyes. 'Then I got what I wanted. Or at least I thought I did,' she blurted. 'That's why my relationships never work. I'm being punished for . . . what I wanted.' A lump rose in Gina's throat and she looked down into her lap.

Jen sighed. 'Oh love, I'm so sorry.' She reached out and put a hand on Gina's arm, squeezing it as Gina looked out over the harbour, the clanging of metal from the docks echoing in the background.

'It doesn't work like that. Sometimes these things just . . . happen. It happens to a lot of women.' Gina shook her head.

'It does. It happened to me.'

Gina looked back, eyes wide and unblinking as Jen reached for her cigarette pack.

'Before Vera, obviously.' Jen pulled out a cigarette and lit it, leaning one arm on the table. 'He'd be twenty, now.' Jen blew out the smoke and shook her head. 'I drank a lot, after he died, so the husband left.' Jen fixed her with a tear-filled gaze. 'A few years later, I was sitting at home, broke, about to be evicted, when I wondered what my son would think of me. Would he have wanted me to ruin my life, or would he have wanted me to be grateful that he came to me, even for a short time?' She shrugged.

Gina bit her lip. 'I'd never thought of it that way. Being grateful I had her those few months . . .'

The red hibiscus plant already looked at home in Gina's garden. Flowers stretching to the sun, they seemed to say, 'I'm fine.' Gina swallowed and hoped it wasn't wishful thinking.

'Okay, first put your message in the hole, and then put the tree on top. Then if you want, say a few words and we can release the balloons,' said Jen.

Vera put the small shovel down on the ground and stood by Gina's side.

Gina nodded. She thought she would cry at this point, but all her tears had been shed in the bath, in the car, and all over her work documents over the past days. It felt like they would never stop. Then one day, she was done. Done with the guilt. Done with the shame. And done with the blame.

She had to let go of the guilt if she was to make good on her promise to the baby she lost. Guilt would only stop her from finding a man who would give her a second chance at having the family she wanted so badly.

It didn't mean she loved her baby any less.

Gina released the balloons, watching them drift up into the cloudless blue sky. 'Come back to me,' she whispered, swallowing as they danced out of sight.

A Window Named Will.

Chapter Twenty Six

Back in Manchester, Will's path to romance had been equally fraught. He had developed a magnetic pull of gold-diggers. Once women saw the car he drove, or he told them where he worked, they became obsessed with going to expensive restaurants and shopping trips.

Lara had potential though. A twenty-eight-year-old TV presenter, she was fun, attractive and could hold a conversation. But their third date, a double with Phoebe and Hamish, as not going as planned.

Will tried not to show how annoyed he was when Lara flirted with the barman. He also tried not to show his concern about the amount she was drinking. For a woman of her slight build, her body would be struggling to process the alcohol she'd imbibed so far – and she had to be at the studio at 4 a.m. tomorrow. Yes it was her choice how much she drank, but she was starting to slur her words, and her head kept nodding forward.

He had to say something.

'I think you should eat something now,' Will urged in a low voice.

'I'm fine.' Lara pushed back her chair and tried to stand, almost falling in the attempt. Will darted up out of his seat, but Phoebe was already by Laura's side, arm firmly around her waist. She nodded at Will to sit down. 'Might be time to call it a night, love,' she said to Lara. 'You have to be right for work in the morning.'

Will sighed as they walked away.

'Hang in there.' Hamish gave him an encouraging smile.

'I don't know. This online dating doesn't seem to be

working.' Will sipped his pint.

'Oh come on, I bet we can find at least five potential dates for you right now.'

Will groaned. 'Slave driver.'

Hamish laughed. 'Yeah, poor you, being forced to find the woman of your dreams. Wait, I'll just get my violin.' He took Will's phone.

Will smiled despite himself and glanced out the window, where Phoebe was putting Lara into a taxi.

'What about her?' Will peered at the screen, smiling as he gazed at the photo of a brunette with sparkling eyes. Lucy, thirty five, Port Moresby. In this photo she was on a sailing boat, fully clothed. 'She's wearing clothes, for a start. You'd be amazed at the pictures people put up on their profiles.'

Hamish grinned. 'So what was Lara's photo like?'

Will grinned.

'Serves you right then, mate.'

Will moved out of the range of Hamish's playful punch, his heart warming as he looked back at Lucy's photo. *Maybe there is hope for me.*

And I thought my luck was changing. Gina rearranged the ice back on her ankle, the TV flickering mutely from the opposite wall. She'd tried running around the yacht club after work, the only safe place available; but with the heat lingering well beyond 5 p.m., she'd lasted ten minutes before heading inside to the club for a drink. So she'd switched to a morning run instead, but the semi-dark and cooler temperatures had been her undoing.

'Men.' Gina leaned back against the sofa cushions and closed her eyes. *If Sean was still here, I wouldn't be running for exercise.* A smile played on her lips as she imagined the aerobic activity she'd like to be enjoying with Sean, but faded as reality dawned. *I can dream, I suppose.* She sighed. *I should have just wallowed in movies and junk food, which I'm doing now, anyway. Hmm, wonder if there are any Twisties left?*

Beep.

Gina opened her eyes and picked up her phone, heart racing. *Is it him?* Her finger hovered over the email icon, and she took a deep breath and clicked.

Not from Sean. Her chest constricted with irritation as she saw yet another notice from the online dating site. She'd planned to close it down, but between *The List*, the carjacking and Sean, she'd forgotten. 'What gem do you have for me now?' Gina grunted and pushed the thoughts of Travis to the back of her mind. But as she read Will's profile, a slow smile spread across her face.

A day later, Gina's sore ankle was all but forgotten.

Gina: *Does your skipper swear as much as mine? It's like going back in time to press-ganged navy days sometimes.*

Will: *It's the sailor's code – no politically correct people allowed. You could wear your grass skirt on board, lighten the mood?*

Gina: *Actually I prefer a bikini*☺ She photo-shopped a picture of a cartoon duck wearing a bikini on to a sailing boat and pressed send.

Will: *Touché*☺

Gina's computer beeped as a message came through from Will. It was a picture of a muscle-bound man in a grass skirt and coconut bra.

Gina: *I hope you only wear that in the summer months over there. Or do you have matching wellies and a brolly?*

Will: *Now that's just cruel, Lucy, not all of us are lucky enough to have tropical warmth and sunshine to perfect an over-all, year-round tan. We Brits have to rely on carcinogenic spray tans, especially here in the North where oompa loompa orange is the preferred skin colour.*

Gina burst out laughing.

Will: *Fancy a Skype chat? No bikinis I promise.*

Gina: Love to ☺

Gina snapped her laptop shut, her cheeks sore from smiling. They'd been messaging for three hours – and he'd not hesitated to flirt with her.

Unlike someone else.

Gina glared at the flashing prawn on her bookshelf. On, off; on, off; just like the man who'd given it to her.

It wasn't good enough. No matter how she felt when she was with him, he'd disappointed her too, like the rest of the men she'd dated.

'You had your chance,' she muttered, turning back to the screen to reread her chat with Will. She'd been tempted to message Sean and tell him about her failed running attempt, but he would see it for what it was: a feeble attempt at making contact again.

And it was up to him to reach out to her, now. She was done with making excuses for the men she dated – even Sean.

The next night, Gina fiddled with her wineglass, pursing her lips to hide her smile. Vera and Jen had arrived, cooked meal in hand, to cheer her up.

'So who is he?' Jen landed on the dining room chair with a thud.

'Who?' Gina asked wide-eyed with mock surprise, with a quick wink at Vera, who was standing behind Jen and shaking her head.

'Oh come on, you don't glow like that unless you're getting some.'

'Weeell, there is someone . . .'

'See, I knew it.' Jen turned to Vera before looking back at Gina and giving her a regal 'please, continue' roll of the hand.

'I met him online. Will – he's British. Our first conversation went on for *two hours*. He's funny, and handsome . . .' Gina shrugged. Hours flew by without noticing, and she always wanted more. She bit her lip.

'Good. I'm glad. So, what next?' Jen turned her face away to blow her cigarette smoke towards the open balcony door. A cool breeze blew in, making the curtains dance towards them, and drifting the cigarette smoke back in Jen's face.

Gina sighed. 'Who knows? But for once, I'm happy to just enjoy the ride.'

Jen made a choking sound. 'Tough when you're not even in the same room.'

The meaning sank in and Gina's jaw fell open. 'Cheeky!' She swatted the air in front of her in a dismissive wave.

'Good to see you smiling again.' Jen ladled a serving of lasagne on to her plate, the scent of melted cheese and basil making Gina's mouth water.

'How can I not smile when you bring me delicacies like this?' She grinned and looked down at the table, cheeks flushing. She should be worried about Will, given the false starts she'd had so far.

But she wasn't.

If she had to provide evidence for what she felt, she'd struggle to do so; but the lightness deep down in her belly, and in her chest, told her what she needed to know.

She was on the right path.

Have I Met My Dream Man?

1. Dark hair – no, but nice anyway – Check.

2. Taller than me (logistics matter) – Check.

3. Wants a relationship and a family (rather than a fling, friends-with-benefits or variation of) – Check and check.

4. Isn't a cyclist or a triathlete (why are they all nuts? Besides, someone who is more worried about his calorie intake than me and who shaves his legs is too effeminate) – Check.

5. Has a job (failed businessmen trying to 'find themselves' need not apply. Do I look like an ATM?) – Check.

6. No Geminis – why do the ones I date always have a psycho personality as their part of their twin nature? – Check.

Woo hoo!

Chapter Twenty Seven

Dear Ms Trent,

My name is Harriet Westworth from Hall and Westworth publishers in the UK.

We are very interested in your work and would like to discuss the possibility working with you to publish a book.

Gina sat up from the lounge and read the sentence again. And again, to be sure.

Someone wants to offer me a book deal?

Her mouth stretched into a smile. Meeting Will and a book deal? Her luck really *was* changing.

'Will again?' Jen smiled at her from the opposite lounge, where she attempted to crochet a string bag. Vera was cleaning out the apartment, and given that Jen tried to keep everything Vera wanted to get rid of, she'd been banished to Gina's.

'Gina why don't you go to the UK and meet with her? You need a break. *And* you could meet someone else while you're there,' Vera suggested with a wink.

Gina nodded and looked at the plastic prawn on the shelf. It was no longer flashing. Much like Sean's feelings for her, it seemed. They'd barely spoken since he'd left for Afghanistan, and initially she'd been understanding. He was starting a new posting. But she'd worked with plenty of military men and they'd managed to email and call from Afghanistan.

Then there was Will, who was consistent *and* keen; two things Sean was not. *We can't Skype forever. Besides, life is too short.* Her thoughts flashed back to the guns pointing at her. She'd been lucky that day; and she'd been given a second chance at life.

Time to make use of it.

'You're right. I'll do it.'

On the other side of the world, Will sat at a bar with a beer in hand under Hamish's quizzical eye.

'She's got you, mate,' Hamish said, following with a playful punch on the arm.

Will shrugged and smiled into his pint. Was he just excited about the online romance, or was there something truly there between them? After Naomi, he wanted to be sure. He *needed* to be sure.

'We've been friends since kindergarten, so I think I can tell.'

'Right,' Will replied, trying not to grin. He thought about Gina all day, even dreamed about her—and if Hamish was noticing, he really had fallen for her.

His chest tightened. Falling for her meant she could hurt him, like Naomi had.

But she's not Naomi.

It was a conversation he'd been having with himself often of late; another sign of how he truly felt. His chest tightened.

'So besides being gorgeous, she's . . .'

Will exhaled, his chest easing as he thought of Gina's smile, her laugh, the way she tilted her head when she thought. 'Talented, interesting . . .'

Roll of the eyes from Hamish.

'She's beautiful.' *Inside, and out.*

Hamish raised an eyebrow, just as Will's phone beeped. A Skype message.

Hi Will, I'm coming to England. Would you like to meet? Gina.

Will couldn't stop the grin from spreading across his face.

'What's up? Did she send you a naughty text? Let me see.' Hamish tried to grab the phone, but Will pulled it out of his reach.

'She's coming to England.'

'It's a sign.' Hamish stood up and patted his back pocket. 'Next round's on me.'

Chapter Twenty Eight

'I am so sorry.' Gina picked up the last of her lipsticks from rolling across the counter of Hall and Wentworth's reception desk. How her handbag had popped open when she put it on the desk, she couldn't understand. But it was just her luck.

'Perfectly all right. Happens to me all the time.' The receptionist gave her a warm smile. 'I'll inform Harriet you're here. Please sit down.'

'Thank you.' Gina checked the zip of her bag before easing into one of the low, cream-leather tub chairs.

Maybe my luck has run out, she panicked. *Maybe nothing has changed for me.*

She took a slow breath in through her nostrils, like Sean had taught her to after the carjacking.

Don't think about that now.

She'd been confident about her decision to travel to the UK until she boarded the plane, her doubts assuaging her since she could no longer turn back. *If Sean didn't want you, Will won't, either. They all disappear once they get to know you.* On and on the thoughts had gone, until she'd been so exhausted she'd fallen into a fitful sleep.

Perhaps she should have delayed her meeting until she'd recovered from the jetlag.

She sighed. *It's done. Just do your best.* She ran through the key messages she'd written on the plane; her work was constantly edited in the public service, so she was used to working with an editor. She was hard working. She had ten thousand followers on Facebook.

But her messages would be hollow if she didn't believe in herself.

She'd seen many a lawyer lose a case because they'd

delivered their arguments without being convincing.

Gina took a deep breath. *I can do this. I have to do this. It's not just for me.*

She swallowed. If she really wanted to change her life, this was her chance.

And if she secured the book deal, it would be a sign that her future lay in England.

Because it certainly didn't involve Sean.

'Ms Trent, come this way please.'

Gina stood, squared her shoulders, and strode after the receptionist.

A half hour later, Gina was shaking Harriet's hand. 'Ms Trent, we would love to work with you. We are looking for authors who are *real* women – not flibbertigibbets.' Harriet's cherry-red lips parted to reveal a set of brilliant white teeth. 'However, this will be a full-time task. You won't be able to continue working.'

Gina kept her lips stretched into a smile. *Of course.* But she couldn't live in Port Moresby unless her employer paid her accommodation.

She'd have to go home to Australia, then, which was even further from England. What would that mean for her and Will?

Harriet frowned at her, and Gina forced herself to grin. She needed to exude confidence, and a 'can do' attitude. 'I'll take care of it.'

Harriet smiled. 'You have the air of a woman who has been negotiating book deals for years. *You're* no flibbertigibbet.'

Gina's eyebrows shot upward. Harriet's directness was a refreshing change from her politically correct public service colleagues who didn't even dare to laugh at jokes in case they appeared insensitive. She would be wonderful to work with.

'And good luck with Will.' Harriet winked.

Chapter Twenty Nine

Good luck with Will. She needed it.

Gina stretched her fingers out, inspecting the pale pink polish she'd applied an hour before. All the way to Manchester on the train, she'd wondered what she would do when they met.

He would be here in moments. Not on a screen, but here, beside her.

You couldn't get a real sense of chemistry when you talked to someone through a screen, since pheromones didn't travel through Skype.

Gina tried to swallow, but her mouth was dry. If she didn't like him, she could just feign illness, and end the evening early.

It wouldn't be a portent of future disaster. It would just be a sign she'd come further along on her journey to finding the life she wanted, but wasn't quite there.

She glanced at the hotel's revolving glass doors, heart beating faster. Older couple, not him.

Teenagers, not him.

Oooh – man in suit. Blond hair askew. A kind smile as he spotted her.

It was him!

Gina stood, heart skittering in her chest.

'You look exactly like your photo.' Will kissed her on the cheek, a soft, gentle kiss that made her heart slow to a steady rhythm. Somehow, that first physical contact confirmed her view of Will. He was the same kind, funny man she'd gotten to know. And she felt sure he wasn't going to hurt her.

He'd passed the pheromone test. She exhaled with

relief. 'So do you.' Gina beamed at him, before biting her lip like a shy child. His cologne was woody and masculine; unlike the citrus-based scents her other dates preferred. It seemed more mature, somehow. Or perhaps it was just the effect of the easy confidence that Will radiated.

'I thought we might head out for dinner. Do you like Italian?' Will's eyes searched hers, his mouth bearing a slight smile. He was sure she'd say yes, she could tell. And he wanted her to say yes, too.

Gina nodded. 'I *love* Italian.' Her mind whirred as soon as she'd spoken the words. *Love. You shouldn't mention the L word on the first date.*

But Will just smiled back at her. 'Great. I know a place I think you'll love.'

Their eyes met, and their smiles broadened at the same moment.

Will took her hand and guided her out on to the street, and it took all her restraint not to break into a skip. She was finally with Will, and he was everything she'd imagined. She snuck a look at him from the corner of her eye: well-cut suit, flat stomach, judging by the way his shirt lay against his waist. She looked towards the ground. His shoes looked handmade.

Good looking, with dress sense. *So far, so good.*

'What do you think of Manchester so far?'

'I love it.' Gina bit her lip. There it was, the L word again. What was it about him that made her keep saying it?

'I'm glad.' He pressed her hand, and winked at her, making her laugh. And what was it about him that made her smile and laugh so much? She turned to look at him, hoping the answer would come to her, when Will pulled her towards his chest.

'Don't get squashed before we have dinner. I don't want

to lose you when you're finally here,' he whispered. Traffic whooshed past, tyres swishing on the wet street, and people milled around them, waiting.

She hadn't even heard the traffic signal change; she'd been so absorbed in him.

Gina looked into his eyes, a sense of calm flowing through her, and her smile faded.

He was perfect. And she knew things would never be the same.

Will sat back in the cane chair and sipped his wine while Gina went to the ladies room of his favourite Italian restaurant. He'd been attracted to her before; but in person, her energy, her laugh, and her dancing eyes made his heart skip a beat.

He was head-over-backside for her, but he wouldn't rush. *This* time, he'd get it right.

How long would she be? Will checked his watch – nearly five minutes since she'd gone to the ladies. He tapped his foot. She hadn't left, had she?

Crash.

'I'm so sorry, I didn't see you.' Gina's face was bright red, as was the face of the waiter who now wore caviar on his shirt.

'Excuse me, madam.' The waiter hurried away.

Will laughed, grateful for a distraction from his earlier worries. 'How was the caviar?' He chuckled as he held her chair out for her.

'Oh, I am so embarrassed!' Gina shook her head, looking at him out of the corner of her eye. If she looked at him that way again, he'd forget his plan to take this relationship slowly.

He smiled. 'Don't be. I do it all the time.'

A blush rose on Gina's cheeks.

'I don't believe that for a second.'

Will laughed. She couldn't be more different to the other women he'd dated. They'd been nice enough, but there was an ingenuity about them, too, he realised now. Gina, however, blurted out what came to mind. And the way her obvious delight in things showed on her face made him want to surprise and impress her for as long as he could.

He sat up taller in his seat. If things went well, perhaps he could make her smile for the rest of her life.

Chapter Thirty

The next day, Will gripped Gina's hand, chest expanding as he gazed at her smiling face. Normally he would wait a few days between dates.

This time, though, he'd jettisoned his usual, relaxed dating strategy.

He couldn't wait days to see her again; couldn't wait to hold her hand in his, smell the gentleness of the rose perfume that lingered in the air around her, or to feel, with every breath, every look and every touch, that he had finally found what he'd been looking for.

He was in trouble – of the best sort.

'How glorious. This is precisely how I imagined an English village to be.' There it was again, that small smile, which made him think of anything but sightseeing.

But it wouldn't do to sleep with her straight away. They at least had to have three dates, in his mind, before it was gentlemanly to even consider seducing her. He knew that dinner and a full day together wasn't technically three dates, but, looked at in terms of hours, he hoped it might prove acceptable to Gina, at least.

If he could get through the day without trying to ravish her. 'Chester is one of my favourite places.' Will grinned, hoping his earlier thoughts weren't obvious. 'And also popular with rich footballers.' That was okay, good tour-guide talk; no sexual innuendo.

'Like in *Soccer Spouses*?' Gina asked with an excited clap. 'I loved that show,' she giggled.

Will took her hand and kissed it. That giggle. Naughty and nice all at once. And she kept using 'love' about everything. He'd usually bristle if a woman mentioned it too early in their romance, but with Gina, he could sense there was no agenda; no attempt to rush him into feeling more than he did.

His eyes locked with hers. 'I love it too.' There, he'd said the L word too. They were even.

He stopped himself from shaking his head. Trying to keep up with how many times she said love!

He'd heard of couples getting married within days of meeting, and always thought it madness. Until now.

He squeezed her hand, and hoped she would say yes to what he had planned for the evening.

Will held open the door of his Jaguar, bringing Gina's thoughts back to the present. Money had never been important to her, but Will used his to enjoy life, something she did too infrequently. When she'd hesitated about having an expensive lunch, he'd simply said 'let me treat you. It will make me happy.'

He was as close to Prince Charming as one would find in real life.

She peeked at him out of the corner of her eye as he closed the door for her. Usually the early dates left her fretting and analysing every word, look, action and inaction but she'd been too busy having fun for any of it.

She glanced over at him, and their eyes met.

There was no need to say anything. He felt it, too.

After a drive of companionable silence intermingled with charged looks and spicy repartee, Will held his front door open for her.

Don't look too eager. He didn't need to know that she'd mentally undressed him throughout the drive, imagining the feel of his chest as she raked her fingertips across them, then unbuttoned his belt and . . .

'What are you smiling at?' Will closed the door behind him cocked an eyebrow at her.

Gina shrugged. 'Wouldn't you like to know.'

'I would, actually.' In two steps he had her in his arms; and his scent, a mix of cashmere and cologne, only added to her desire.

I want you. She almost said the words out loud, when Will scooped her off her feet and carried her up the stairs.

Chapter Thirty One

Gina opened a cautious eye the next morning, and was greeted by the sight of a breakfast tray, decorated with a red rose.

She smiled and sat up. 'You just keep getting better and better,' she said, pouring herself a cup of steaming hot tea from the pot and looking about the room.

Plush crème carpet covered the floor, and a gold and brown striped duvet hung askew over one corner of the bed. Smoked-glass wardrobe doors ran across the length of the room. The man had a wardrobe most women would envy.

In the corner, an elegant chrome floor lamp hung over a dark leather wing chair, a mahogany side table laden with books to one side.

The sort of bedroom James Bond would approve of. There was no woman's touch here at all, a good sign. Her chest tightened. But there'd been no sign of a woman in Max's apartment, either.

Gina crept out of bed and snuck to the wardrobe, sliding one of the doors back. She waited, one eye on the door; thankful for the wardrobe's silent tracks.

Nothing.

She turned, heart beating in her ears, and scanned rows of empty racks and shelves scuffed by the previous occupant. A sprinkling of silver glitter shone from the carpet, a remnant of a shoe, or dress. She slid the door closed, to see another empty wardrobe, followed by another. At the end, Will's clothes hung in tidy rows.

She slid the door closed, a pang of guilt piercing her stomach.

He wasn't married. But he'd lost someone, and yet he wasn't bitter. He was just . . .

She exhaled.

'Baby you can drive my car boom boom boom boom boom.'

Gina grinned. He was no singer, that's for sure.

She spotted her knickers on the floor by her feet and stooped to pull them on. Her shirt lay crumpled by the curtains, and she pulled it over her head before padding down the stairs and glancing around the sitting room. A large navy fabric sofa faced a wall of white bookcases, at the end of which stood a full suit of armour, polished to a high sheen. The room was flooded with a gentle light from the garden, surrounded by high brick walls covered in English ivy. A neatly clipped lawn was edged by garden beds filled with daffodils. Not a weed in sight.

A loud clanging from the kitchen interrupted her musing. *He's almost as noisy as me in the kitchen,* she thought as she tiptoed over the white shag rug and peeked around the corner of the door jamb. Will's bottom wriggled at her in welcome as he flipped a pancake over, cracking the frying pan against the stove as the pancake came down.

'Damn!'

Gina laughed. 'Thought I heard The Beatles.' She leant against the door jamb and crossed her arms.

Will started and turned around.

'Ah! Good morning, sleeping beauty.' His eyes creased as he grinned, and lifted his spatula. 'I didn't wake you, did I?' A frown settled on his forehead.

'No. I just wanted to see the show.' Gina gave a little wiggle, and Will laughed.

'Oh, that.' A red stain crept up his neck.

'It was cute.' Gina grinned.

'Flattery will get you everywhere.' Will winked at her and turned back to the frying pan.

***

Will lifted the last pancake on to the plate. He'd been unable to sleep, having spent half the night watching Gina bathed in moonlight. How could he sleep when he was seeing his life fall into place, and knew, finally, that he was on the right path.

He wanted her to stay.

But did *she* want to stay?

He knew the sensible thing to do was ask, but she might think him mad asking so early in their relationship.

And if he didn't ask? He might lose her anyway.

He put down the spatula and took a deep breath. Gina was worth taking a risk for.

'These are great!' Gina poured more maple syrup over the half-finished stack of pancakes on her plate.

A warmth spread through Will's chest. It was a sign.

'Gina?'

She looked at him over the fork in her mouth. 'Hmm?' He could hear the smile in her voice.

'What are you doing next?

Gina finished chewing and looked him in the eye. 'Well . . .' She raised her eyebrows.

Will laughed. 'Not that. I mean, yes, I plan to pick up where we left off once we're fed and watered, but . . .' He leant over the table and reached out his hand.

Gina put down her fork and put her hand in his, her eyes searching his face.

'What I mean is, what are you doing after today?'

Gina's brow furrowed.

Oh no. I've spooked her. She thinks I'm some psycho who's trying to trap her too early. Will's heart thudded in his chest.

Then a smile spread across Gina's face. 'I'm planning to travel for a few more weeks. But after that?' She raised her eyebrows at him.

Will tightened his grip on Gina's hand, heart thudding.

'Let me know when you're finished travelling, and I'll be at the airport to pick you up. Maybe you can stay on for a while?'

Gina's smile broadened. 'I'd love to.'

Chapter Thirty Two

Gina sipped her wine and gazed out over St Paul's Bay, a pang of envy stabbing her stomach as a couple strolled past hand-in-hand. *I wish that was us.* She sighed. It had been six weeks since she'd seen Will, escaping to Ireland, Norway and Iceland to consider Will's offer. She'd made enough mistakes with men; so she'd known she'd made a mistake leaving Will as soon as her plane left Manchester. No matter the beauty of her surroundings, she'd been miserable; her thoughts dominated by the man she'd left behind.

Still, she wanted him to consider what he was asking, and the more time they spent apart, the more sure he would be. She hoped.

She smiled as she thought of their ardent lovemaking before she left six weeks ago.

Will. Six weeks.

Coins clattered on to the cobblestones as she paid the bill, then rushed to the nearest chemist. With a pounding heart she picked up a pregnancy kit and took it to the counter. 'Good luck.' The girl smiled as she rang up the purchase and gave Gina her change.

Half an hour later, Gina sat on the bed and placed her hand on her stomach, tears trickling down her cheeks.

A second chance.

'Mr Lockwood?'

Will started, sorting through his papers. Mrs Leavers, his secretary, was no doubt checking he'd had his elevenses, and would be furious when she saw the uneaten scone on the plate, yet again.

'Would you like a sandwich, Mr Lockwood? You haven't eaten all day. And it's nearly two o'clock.' Mrs Leavers sighed as she picked up the scone.

'You're a brick, Mrs Leavers. Maybe egg and cress then,' he replied with what he hoped was a grateful smile.

'Right you are, Mr Lockwood. I might get you a nice custard tart as well, you like them.'

Will sat back in his chair. Food was a poor consolation. He missed Gina so much his heart ached, but he had to give her time. He had to get this right.

His phone rang, and he jumped as Gina's number flashed on the screen. *It's her.* He gulped as he pressed the answer button. 'Gina?'

'Hi.' Her voice was soft, but there was something else there, too.

Worry.

Will clenched his jaw. *Oh no, she's ringing to tell me she's not coming back.* He shook his head. *But I thought I'd done everything right. Asked her to stay, given her time to consider it.*

But it wasn't enough.

He cleared his throat. 'How are you?'

Gina sniffled, making Will grimace. It was definitely bad news if she was crying.

'I'm pregnant, Will. I've done four tests, to be sure.'

Will blinked.

Gina wasn't dumping him?

She was pregnant?

He'd braced himself for bad news but this – this was fantastic!

He knew he should say something reassuring, but his brain couldn't find the words. And the last thing Gina needed was for him to be uncertain. She needed him to be strong for her. He would have to pull himself together. 'Gina, I need to call you back in five minutes. Don't go anywhere.'

Will walked into the men's, loosened his tie, and propped his hands on the basin.

Yes, he'd wanted her to stay, but not because she was pregnant. He sighed. He had to stand by her, and wanted to. But what if she didn't want him? She might think it too much, too soon – and he wouldn't blame her if she did.

It could work, if they wanted it to.

He'd just have to reassure Gina of that.

Will splashed his face with cold water and went back to his desk, but concentrating was useless. The words could have been Cantonese for all he knew, they were just as jumbled as the thoughts rushing through his head.

Do the right thing.

I'm going to be a dad.

But I'm not ready to be a dad.

His gaze rested on the rain-drenched street below, where a little girl beamed as she splashed through the puddles.

Will looked down at his hands, still bare of a wedding ring. He was forty four. It could be his last chance.

When Mrs Leavers returned, he was pulling on his jacket.

'Thanks, Mrs Leavers, I'll take it with me in the taxi. Must dash.' He smiled as he took the bag she handed him.

Two hours later he was on a plane bound for Malta.

Chapter Thirty Three

Gina twisted the hem of her dress. Will had sounded shocked when she told him, which was understandable – but then he'd insisted on coming to see her.

And that could only mean he wanted to deliver bad news.

How would he tell her? she wondered. Say it's too much, too soon?

She sighed. *I should have known he was too good to be true.*

Gina cast a longing gaze towards the bottle of wine she'd bought the other day, licking her lips and jumping as the taste of the wine she'd drunk at lunch registered on her taste buds. 'I'm sorry, I didn't know.' Gina placed a hand on her belly. 'I hope you're okay there, little one.' She looked down at her stomach. There was no sign of the life within, but already, she felt love in a way she'd thought she never would again.

It doesn't matter what he says. I have you. And that's more than enough for me.

Will's heart pounded as Gina opened the door of her room, staring at him with a defiant gaze. Her eyes were red, but otherwise, she looked no different since he last saw her. He frowned, both at the signs of her tears and the fact that she didn't look visibly changed. Weren't pregnant women supposed to feel sick?

'Come in.' Gina turned and he followed her into the room, letting the door close after him.

'It's not very fancy, but I wanted to save my money for sightseeing.'

Will cast an eye around the sparse room, raising an

eyebrow at the vinyl settee Gina sat down on. 'I'm not here to talk about the room, Gina.'

She glanced up at him and bit her lip.

'How are you feeling?' he asked, frowning as he sat beside her.

Gina peered at him, her eyes widening as his meaning registered. 'Oh. Well, no morning sickness yet, if that's what you mean.'

'I thought you'd look . . . different, somehow.'

Gina gave a low laugh. 'I think that comes later.' Her eyes sparkled as she looked at him, her earlier hesitation melting into shy warmth.

'Oh. Right.' Their eyes locked, and Will almost sighed with relief. So far, so good. 'I've missed you,' he said, his mouth stretching into a small smile.

'I missed you too. But I didn't want to say anything. Didn't want you to feel overwhelmed.'

'Me overwhelmed by you missing me?' Will shook his head and pulled her into an embrace. 'Never.' He closed his eyes, inhaling the musky scent of her hair. Babies smelt good too, sometimes, he mused, remembering the baby smell of Hamish's children.

He opened his eyes, and Gina looked up at him. 'What do you want to do?' Will held his breath as he scanned her eyes. *Please, please say yes.*

Gina swallowed. 'I . . . I want to keep the baby.' Gina's chin wobbled. 'But if you don't, then . . .'

Had he heard right? She wanted him, and the baby? He scanned her face, heart swelling as Gina bit her lip. He leaned in and kissed her forehead. 'That's good, because I wasn't planning to leave without you.'

A slow grin spread across Gina's face. 'Really?'

He nodded. 'Really.' He kissed her again. He wasn't sure how their relationship would turn out, no one could be, but they wanted to be together and start their family. And that was all that mattered.

Chapter Thirty Four

Gina stared at the bookshelf in Will's living room, the titles of his books blurring in front of her weary eyes. Her baby book lay open at the same page she'd been reading twenty minutes ago.

She used to speed read for work, now, she couldn't even read five pages without a nap. She smiled. Napping during the day – she'd dreamed about doing that when she worked. She looked at the computer screen, a pang of guilt stabbing at her chest. By rights she should be working on her novel outline, but with the move, morning sickness and adjusting to living with Will, she'd not had the energy to be creative.

Gina cradled her belly, glancing at the bunch of flowers Will sent earlier that day.

She finally had everything she'd dreamed of having. A wonderful man, a baby, and a new career as a writer – everything except peace. A niggling voice persisted in whispering to her, in silent moments: *Is it too good to be true? Sean left you, didn't he? And Alex. And Max. What's to say Will won't leave you, too?* Her breath caught in her chest.

As if on cue, the front door rattled. 'Hiya.' The familiar clatter of an umbrella being placed in the stand, keys tumbling into the bowl and the swish of a jacket being hung up eased Gina's breathing. Just being in Will's presence dispelled her cloudy thoughts. She beamed as Will walked over to her and kissed the top of her head.

'You look so cute with your glasses.' He sat down beside her, pulling her to him and nuzzling her neck.

Gina giggled and squirmed out from the ticklish onslaught. 'Really?'

'I'm not in the habit of wasting words, young lady,' he said, pulling her back into a hug. He tapped the tip of her nose with his finger. 'I've a surprise for you.'

Gina frowned. *Making love is the last thing I feel like doing.*

'No, not that.' He laughed. 'I'd like you to meet my mother.'

Gina stiffened, and Will narrowed his eyes as he peered at her. 'That's not a problem is it? I mean, you're not having second thoughts . . .'

Gina's chest tightened. They hadn't told her parents yet, or Will's mum. No point telling them if their relationship failed.

More than once she'd urged herself to 'go with the flow', 'think positive', and many other mantras to induce confidence in her good fortune – but it would only make her deepest fear surface.

You don't deserve to be a mother.

If only she could talk to Will about it, he would know what to say. He could always convince her out of her worries.

She looked away from Will's face, concentrating hard on the carpet fibres to keep back the nascent tears. *I can't tell him. I can't risk losing his love.* Gina looked back at Will, giving him the best smile she could manage. 'No, I'm not having second thoughts.' She reached out and took his shirt in her fingers, sliding the fabric through them. 'But I keep thinking it's too good to be true. That something bad will happen between us.' Tears sprang to her eyes.

'Oh, sweetheart.' Will's brow furrowed. 'I'm not going anywhere. Okay?' Will squeezed her to him.

'I know,' she said, her voice small, and tentative. 'What

if your mother doesn't like me, though?' His mother
might sense her deception and her doubts. Gina
swallowed.

'She'll love you. If I'm happy, she's happy.'

'And . . . are you . . . happy?' She turned and looked up
at him, her eyes searching his.

'Yes, I am,' he said, kissing her forehead, before his
brow furrowed. 'Are you?'

'Of course I am.' She cupped his cheek in her palm.
'How could I not be?'

Will put his hand on hers. 'So what's troubling you?'

Gina sighed and let her hand slide from Will's cheek.
Should I tell him? She looked into his eyes, soft with such
love. No. It would be selfish. Will would only worry, and
he had enough to worry about with the business, and
becoming a father. Besides, there were plenty of other
concerns she could talk to him about; things he *could*
actually fix. Her career, the reaction of her parents . . . 'I
haven't made any progress with the book yet. I need to
decide what to do with my job longer term. And I don't
know what to say to my parents.'

Will took her hands in his. 'I'll book us in to see my
lawyer, and sort out a new visa. And your parents will be
thrilled. Trust me.'

Gina gave Will a half smile. *He's so certain,* she
thought, squeezing his hands. *But he can't promise that
things will turn out okay this time.* She glanced down at
her belly. *No one can.*

Will pulled her hands to his lips and kissed them. 'I will
take care of you both. You needn't worry. I promise.'

Gina nodded, smile widening. Will's optimism was
infectious; one of the many reasons she loved him. She
leant forward and placed a soft kiss on his lips. 'Good. I'm
going to hold you to that.'

***

Sean pounced on Vera's email, one of many which had piled up while his internet connection had been down. He'd been waiting on this response to his deliberately casual email, with its offhand comment about Gina's travels. She was obviously keen on this man she'd met, if she was going to visit him in England. His stomach tensed as he clicked on the message. He'd tried to hide from the possibility Gina was truly lost to him, but the uncertainty had been worse than he'd imagined. He'd slept poorly, lost his appetite, and been unable to think about anything but Gina for weeks.

He had to know.

But as he scanned Vera's reply, he wondered whether he'd made the right choice.

Jen is heading to the UK to visit Gina, to make sure she and the baby are okay.

Sean sat back in his chair. *Gina pregnant?* He glanced back at the email. Gina had left work and moved to England, and was living with *him*. Will Lockwood.

Blood pumped through his muscles, and he paced to the wall. He wanted to hit something, or someone — preferably Will, if he'd been close enough. Not that it was Will's fault though, it was his own. *I'm an idiot. I should have taken a risk. And now . . .* Sean raised his fist and slammed it into the wall, recoiling as plaster splintered to the floor in a sprinkling of white dust.

He blinked, staring at his hand in the wall.

What are you doing? He pulled his hand from the newly formed hole, coughing as the dust spread. *Getting angry won't bring her back, will it, you goose?* He looked at his bleeding knuckles and shook his head. *And how are you going to explain this when you put in the maintenance request?*

Sean stepped back and slumped into the soft leather of the chair, staring at the wall. The last time he'd punched something, it had been a punching bag. He'd never lashed out in anger before.

He closed his eyes, ignoring the stinging cuts on his hand.

He could hit as many walls as he pleased, but it wouldn't bring Gina back to him.

Verity Laschelle was in the habit of getting what she wanted. And she wanted Sean.

She had been working on him since arriving in Afghanistan; asking him to help her with at work, to show her around the gym, and working the damsel in distress routine overtime. He could see it coming and could have avoided it if he'd wanted to. But after snooping on Will and discovering he was handsome, wealthy, and accomplished, he'd sought her out, knowing where the evening would end. Verity wasn't after a boyfriend, and he wasn't looking for a girlfriend. Not anymore.

'So Sean, do you have a girlfriend?' asked Verity as she toyed with her drink.

Sean tried not to stare at her ample cleavage positioned strategically in her tight top. Gina was happy with someone else. No point pining for her. Move on.

'No, I don't.' He put thoughts of Gina aside, and leaned in to kiss Verity.

Chapter Thirty Five

Gina watched the rows of homes pass by in silence. Stately mansions were set back from the street, many with ivy-clad walls and long drives. If Will's mother lived in a house like this, she'd no doubt be proper.

What if I use the wrong fork or spoon? She bit her lip, imagining Will's mother glaring at her, lips pursed as she sipped tea from gold-rimmed china. The houses that they zipped past were at least ten times larger than the house she grew up in, and far grander. Will's mother would sense that on sight, and be sure to urge Will to find someone of his own class.

'Why so quiet?' Will asked, his voice soft.

Gina swallowed past the lump in her dry throat. 'Nerves.'

Will looked back to the road, but the corner of his mouth turned up as he smiled. 'My mother is not a tyrant. And we don't live in a pile like these places.' He jerked his head at the window.

'Oh.' Gina exhaled, and Will gave a low chuckle as they drove down the high street. Shops with shining windows and bright displays lined the road, and Gina counted at least three bakeries, a pub, a butcher, and a pound store. She smiled. Who'd have thought to find a pound store in a village? She felt more at home already.

Will slowed as they neared a T-intersection and turned right, past a church overlooking an expanse of field dotted with camel-coloured cows who looked at her with mournful, dark eyes. *Good luck,* they seemed to say.

Gina's hands shook, and she folded them together.

Will's mother had to be lovely – she'd raised Will, after all. *You're worrying about nothing,* she reminded herself, yet again.

After a row of picturesque houses, Will turned the car into a neat, gravel drive. 'Here we are. See? Nothing grand about it.'

Gina leaned forward and peered out the windscreen. The two-storey house looked almost double the size of her own childhood home. Topped with a thatched roof, its white walls gleamed in the gentle light. Two topiary trees lined the black front door, their red ceramic pots pristine. Everything was neat, beautiful, and spoke of a love of detail; a standard she could only hope to meet in her own life.

Gina wrung her hands together as Will pulled up by the door. This house emanated glamour, and she was far from glamorous. She glanced down at her dress. She'd bought it especially for the visit: soft pink, with plenty of draping fabric that gave her an air of elegance. She only hoped Will's mother liked it.

'She'll love you. Relax.' Will leaned over and kissed her, when her door opened.

'Ma chérie!' A small, thin woman, with short, grey hair coiffured into elegant waves, stood before her, smiling. Her lavender eyes shone with happiness and sincerity. Gina pulled her knotted fingers apart, letting them relax in her lap. *Not what I was expecting – and thank goodness for that.*

'Mother, at least let her out of the car.' Will exited the car and his mother darted towards him, kissing him on both cheeks. 'You look more handsome every time I see you.'

Gina slid out of the car and straightened her dress, grateful for the delay.

'You're right, she is beautiful.' Will's mother faced her

now, and Will winked at Gina over his mother's shoulder. His mother held her arms open to her, and Gina dutifully stepped into her embrace, surrounded in a halo of hairspray and gentle, floral perfume.

Gina's cheeks flushed as Will's mother took her arm in hers. 'I'm Elly, no standing on ceremony here.' Elly patted her hand. 'After all, you're family now.'

Gina's eyes misted with tears. Family.

Her heart swelled as gratitude.

'I have some tea for you.' Elly ushered her into a sitting room, and Gina took a covert glance around the room. Polished wood cabinets filled the room, topped with doilies and dainty china figurines. Photographs, some in old frames, lined the walls: a wedding photo – Elly and Will's father, perhaps? Another of a smiling young boy, with dimples. Will. Gina's mouth eased into a smile.

The room was cosy, and stuffed full of memories and beloved items. Just like her parents' house.

Just like home.

'You must be hungry, non?' Elly showed her to the sofa, perching herself in front of a tray laden with plates of scones, biscuits, cake, and sandwiches. She put her hand on an elegant crème teapot decorated with burgundy and pink flowers.

Gina bit her lip to hide her grin. An abundance of food – definitely just like home.

Will laughed as he entered the room. 'We just had breakfast. Why don't I read through those papers you mentioned on the phone, and you show Gina around?' He nodded at Gina. *Okay?*

Gina nodded back, before giving Elly a broad smile. 'I'd like to do your delicious cooking justice.'

Elly's eyes sparkled. 'Of course, as you wish.' She took her hand from the handle of the teapot. 'Then, I shall show you something.' They stood, and Elly held out her hand to Gina, wrapping her small fingers around Gina's. The warm softness of her grip made fresh tears spring to Gina's eyes. So much kindness enveloped her in this family, which made her new life even more perfect – and even more precious.

With slow steps they made their way up a wide, carpeted staircase, and Gina surveyed the polished oak dados, a watercolour of a man fishing by a lake, and more family portraits. The house was a happy home, and despite Elly being its only resident, still felt warm and lived-in; just the way a grandmother's house should be.

They reached the top of the stairs, and Elly nodded at the door opposite. 'Will's room. Keep out . . .' declared a poster decorated with rocket ships and stars. Gina's heart lurched.

'I couldn't bear to change his room. And he never removed the posters, even when he returned for school holidays.' Elly smiled as she guided her towards the door, opening it and motioning Gina inside.

Gina looked around the room. It didn't look like it had changed from the time Will had been there as a child: cricket gear stood in the corner, and a bag of marbles hung from the handle of the wardrobe. Only a bottle of Will's cologne on the dresser indicated that the room's occupant had grown to manhood.

'Sit.' Elly nodded at the bed, before opening the wardrobe and pulling something down from the overhead shelf. A small, scruffy brown bear, with a bald patch on one elbow. Elly sat beside her on the bed, and held the bear out to her. 'This was Will's first toy,' she said, handing her the bear. 'I kept it for my first grandchild.'

It had a kind smile, just like Will. Will would have looked so adorable as a baby holding this. She could imagine their own child cuddling it, drooling over it, loving it, continuing the tradition.

A tear slid down her cheeks.

'What is it, ma chérie? Do you not like the bear?'

'No, I do.' Gina sniffled. 'It's just . . . a little overwhelming.' She gave a short laugh. 'In a good way.'

Elly shuffled closer and put an arm around her shoulders. 'Ah. That is life, non?' She waved her free hand. 'But the Lord only gives us what he knows we can manage,' she quoted, squeezing Gina closer.

'My grandmother used to say that all the time,' said Gina, dabbing at her tear-stained cheeks with the back of her hand. It was a saying she'd called to mind often just after she lost the baby, and hearing Will's mother say the same thing was yet another good sign.

'Your grandmother was a wise lady. And you must be too, *mon chou*. After all, you picked my son.' Elly grinned.

Gina chuckled. 'I suppose so,' she said, a sense of lightness spreading in her chest.

'The poor love tried to stay awake, but I insisted she rest.' His mother opened the door to let Pepper, the family Labrador, out into the garden. Will cast a glance towards the ceiling for any sign Gina had woken. The way Gina cycled through emotions in a day, it was no wonder she was worn out already. He smiled. *But she thrives on it.*

The kettle clicked and he poured the steaming water into the mugs and stirred the coffee, adding milk and sugar before carrying the mugs out to the garden.

His mother sat down on the white wooden bench by the rose garden. 'I remember when I was pregnant with you. I would fall asleep everywhere. And cry for no reason. But we managed,' she said with a sigh, taking a mug from Will.

Will took a sip of coffee, his gaze resting on the rose

bush his father planted for his mother on their silver wedding anniversary. Every year he planted a new rose, saying that the thorns and flowers were the perfect symbol for marriage. This one was filled with magnificent red blooms which flourished year after year, no matter how hard they were pruned or how bad the frost was; just like the many happy years of marriage his parents had enjoyed.

Would he and Gina be as happy as his parents were? He took another sip. He hoped so, but hope wasn't always enough. He'd never admit it out loud, but for once, he lacked confidence. Would he be a good husband? He wanted to be, but he'd seen many of his friends, good men, who worked hard for their families, blindsided by their wives asking for a divorce. And they'd not seen any sign of trouble until their wife had ended the marriage.

'There is no secret to it, you just need to work at it. To want it.'

Will nodded. 'I do.'

'Then you will be fine.' His mother took a hand from her mug and patted his.

Will's jaw stiffened. He would do all in his power to make Gina happy – he just hoped it would be enough.

Chapter Thirty Six

A loud honk came from the street, and Will peeped out the window. A large truck stretched in front of his house, and those either side. His stomach dropped. They'd agreed Gina would only bring essentials across – this looked like far more than the essentials. 'Lord above.' Luckily most of the neighbourhood was at the Manchester City game, else they'd be blocking the whole street.

'Ooh, I can't wait till you see the day bed.' Gina grinned as she darted to the door.

'Day bed? I thought you were just bringing the essentials?'

Gina frowned. 'I did.'

Will bit back the response on his tongue. It wouldn't do to argue in front of the removalists. Besides, it was done now. He only hoped they'd have room for everything.

Gina flung the door open and raced down the path.

'Morning love.' A removalist opened the doors of the truck, and Will blanched at the sight of boxes stacked from top to bottom.

'Just how many boxes of clothes and shoes are there?'

Gina looked up at him, chin wobbling.

Oh no. He'd done it again. Seemed to say the wrong thing every day of late. 'Gina, I didn't mean anything by it.' One of the removal men smirked at Will, and he raised his eyebrows at him, while pulling Gina into a hug. *Looks like the work has started already.*

Will puffed as he served the squash ball to Hamish. He'd escaped the house to let Gina potter about with her things. There wasn't enough room for him, anyway, it seemed. Rooms were lined with boxes, and the house, which used to feel spacious, now seemed far too small.

It wasn't the same home anymore. And he hated to admit that the change bothered him.

Hamish served the ball back. 'Time to finish up, I think.'

Will nodded, stopping the ball with his racquet and letting it bounce to a standstill. He'd have to face home eventually, but he hoped Hamish might stay for a pint or two at least. If he chugged back lager at home, Gina would know he was annoyed – and that would lead to another argument.

'How did you cope going through this twice? Will asked as walked off the court, packing up their gear.

'You'll forget it with the first hold, and before you know it you'll having your second one,' Hamish said with a laugh as he zipped his bag closed.

Will sighed. 'Maybe. I'm not counting my chickens, though.' He slung his bag over his shoulder and headed to the door.

Hamish frowned at him. 'This isn't like you.' They walked a few paces to the pub next door, and the bar tender nodded as they neared the bar. 'The usual, thanks Ewan.'

Drinks in hand, they sat at a table in the corner, and Will sipped his pint under Hamish's steady gaze.

'Things go all right today?' Hamish asked after what seemed a long period of silence.

Will shrugged. He didn't want to complain any more than he had – it wasn't loyal to Gina. He pursed his lips.

'That good, eh?'

Will put his pint down and stared at the table.

'It's a big step, moving in together.' Hamish glanced at him before dropping his eyes to his pint.

Will gave a small nod.

'And having a baby on the way isn't easy. Not for any man, no matter how long he's been with his partner.'

'Yeah, but does every man get pushed out of his own home?' He regretted the words once he'd said them – it sounded so petty said out loud.

Hamish leant back against the bench. 'How do you think Gina feels? She's changed countries, left her job.' He cocked an eyebrow.

Will's mouth fell open as the kernel of an idea formed. Of course Gina would want her things around her, to give her a sense of home. But how could she feel at home in *his* house? Naomi had nothing when they moved in, but Gina travelled like a pack horse. And it would be disconcerting for a mum-to-be, living in someone else's house rather than one she'd chosen. He remembered Phoebe talking about nesting, or something like that, when she'd redecorated the house before her youngest was born.

His lips spread into a smile.

'That's it!'

Hamish peered at him.

'Maybe it's a sign: time for a family home, rather than a bachelor pad.'

Will closed the front door as softly as he could, hoping the plastic wrap of the flowers wouldn't crinkle and give away his surprise. They were only convenience store flowers, but he hoped Gina liked them, anyway.

'Hi, how did you go?' Gina looked up from her place on the sofa, pulling items from the box beside her.

Will nodded. 'Fine.' His cheeks flushed, and he thrust the flowers forward. 'I bought you these. As a 'welcome home' present.'

Gina looked up at him, lips pursed into a lopsided

smile. 'Oh, you are so sweet.' She took the flowers from him and gazed at them, lips pursing as she stroked the petals of a wilted red rose bud. Will's chest warmed. You'd think she was looking at the most elegant bouquet by the expression on her face. He sat beside her and placed a kiss on her forehead.

'And I have another surprise for you, too.'

Gina placed the flowers on to the table and looked at him with shining eyes, making his chest expand with pride. She'd be even happier once he told her what he planned. He took her hands in his. 'I want to buy a new house. One that we choose together.' He glanced at her belly. 'A family home.'

Gina's mouth fell open. 'But – this one is fine.'

Will laughed. 'It is, but it's not really big enough, is it?' He nodded at the boxes. 'And when the baby comes, we'll need more room again.'

Gina's brow furrowed, and he tried not to smile. You could see the wheels turning in her mind. He knew she'd protest, with her love of saving money, but if it was for the baby, she'd find it hard to argue.

'We could have a play room just for the baby. And a bigger garden.'

Gina glanced at the French doors to the garden. 'True.' She looked back at him. 'Are you sure, Will? I know how much you love this house.'

'There are more important things to consider.' He shrugged, his cheeks warming as Gina gazed at him with such open adoration that his breath caught in his chest.

'I can't believe how lucky I am.' Gina shook her head. 'You are more wonderful every day.' She swallowed, then glanced away.

Will frowned. Had he heard right?

No woman had ever said something like that to him. And Naomi hadn't once shown true appreciation, only a child-like gratitude for the latest shiny object he bought her; whereas Gina kept trying to talk him out of spending money.

A lump rose in Will's throat and he pulled Gina to him, before he burst into tears.

Chapter Thirty Seven

Gina leant back against the soft down pillows, a now empty cup of tea at her side, along with the remnants of toast with margarine. No stomach for vegemite this morning. After years of scoffing breakfast at her desk, breakfast in bed was a welcome change.

As was the view she enjoyed along with her meal.

Gina's eyes caressed Will's back as he pulled on his suit jacket. How did he make such a simple movement so sexy? His muscles rippled as he dipped his right arm into his sleeve, and her mouth watered.

She glanced at the clock on her bedside table. 7:30 – no time for that. A grin parted her lips.

Will turned to her, a smile spreading across his face. 'Wish I didn't have a meeting to rush off to.' He padded over to her, leaning down and kissing her on the forehead. 'Have a good day.'

Gina nodded. 'You too,' she said, voice husky.

'Go back to sleep.' Will stroked her face with his index finger.

Gina reached up and put her hand on his. 'I will, now scoot, before you're late for work. Again.' Will's colleagues had started teasing him about the number of traffic jams he'd encountered of late.

'Bye.' Will winked at her before heading out the door, closing it with a gentle click.

Gina eased herself into the pillows once more, and reached for the laptop Will had brought up for her; chest tensing. Will had told her that inspiration would strike, but still she tried to force the words. She glanced at the boxes stacked in the corner of the room. Maybe he was right; and there was plenty to do while she waited.

She made her way to the first box and put the removals checklist on the floor beside her. If she sorted through these last boxes, she would be sure that everything Jen had packed had been sent before Jen arrived for her visit. Gina had been given strict instructions to report back to Jen if anything was missing, so she could find the items and bring them with her. It wasn't unusual for boxes to be waylaid at the removal depot.

She smiled, imagining the conversation Jen would have with the removal company's staff if anything was missing, when she spotted the words 'private' marked on one of the cardboard flaps.

Her smile faded, and she eased the cardboard apart. Most likely it contained the contents of her filing cabinet, but the way her stomach dropped told her otherwise. With shaking hands she pulled away layers of crumpled brown paper, coughing as dust and dirt swirled up to her face. Still can't escape Port Moresby's dust; she thought with a wry smile. Dropping the paper behind her, she leaned over the box and grimaced as she spotted the grey diary.

Her diaries were bright, or covered in flowers, except one – the one she'd kept after her baby died.

She stood, staring at it, heart thudding in her chest as she touched it with her finger, drawing it back a second after touching the stiff cardboard.

For years she'd read and reread this book, thinking it would keep the memory of her baby alive. Now, a surge of anger welled up from her belly. *It can't happen again.*

She lunged at it, grabbing it by a corner and marching to the office in the room next door. *It can't happen again.*

She sat in Will's large brown leather chair, her muscles flinching at the coldness of the leather, before sitting the book on her lap and wrenching a handful of pages free.

She leant forward and fed the pages into the shredder, its loud whirring sending a rippling of gooseflesh up her arms. Gina gritted her teeth, ripped another bunch of pages from the book, and fed them into the top of the machine; then another and another; finally leaning back against the chair and staring at the shredder.

Maybe I should burn the pieces, just to be sure.

She pulled the lid of Will's shiny metal bin away and cast the contents of the shredder inside, lighting a match from Will's drawer and dropping it on top of the pile of paper. The pieces blackened at the edges and curled inwards, before succumbing to the orange flames that greedily consumed them. Gina watched with a macabre sense of relish, staring until the last piece of paper disappeared.

She leaned against the back of the chair and looked up at the photo on Will's desk. It was a candid photo his mother had snapped of them in her garden; Will was feeding her a piece of cake on a fork. He was beaming, and she was laughing, the fork hovering between them. 'It's my turn to force feed you, for a change,' Will had joked before the photo was taken; and he still made that quip each morning when he brought in her breakfast tray.

Her life was no longer filled with lingering sadness, thanks to Will.

And with him by her side, this time, things would be different.

She glanced at the blackened scraps in the bin. *I'll make sure of it.*

The left side of Hamish's mouth curled up into a grin, and he poured more wine into Will's glass.

'Cut it out, kids,' Hamish yelled as the sound of stomping came from above. 'Kids. See what you've got to look forward to?'

Will frowned at the ceiling.

'So Gina's settling in well, then?' Phoebe asked, raising an eyebrow.

'Seems to be. She does this weird thing of a morning, where she rests her legs up the wall. It's supposed to do something for your immune system,' Will said with a laugh, before glancing at his watch. 'And on that note, I'd better go. Gina's finishing her pregnancy yoga class soon. I don't want to be late to pick her up.'

Phoebe came up behind him and squeezed his shoulders. 'Someone's in luuurve,' she teased.

'Phoebe,' Hamish hissed.

Will swatted her hands away as his dimples creased. Love. Already? Well, he was making Gina breakfast in bed, calling her at lunch time to check how her day was, and fussing over what she did and did not eat. Her worries were now his worries, including one she had not shared.

It was only an innocent slip of the tongue on the doctor's part that made him realise she'd had a miscarriage in the past. Once he knew, he could understand her compulsive researching about pregnancy, and her fixation with her health. She would run to the doctor after a sneeze.

Will looked at the floorboards to hide his nascent tears. Gina hadn't hesitated to stay with him and bear his child. He doubted he could have such faith in anyone after losing a baby as she had.

But she clearly trusted him – and he would not let her down.

Chapter Thirty Eight

Sean put his hand on his knee to stop his leg's nervous tapping against his computer desk. He'd come to the conclusion that Gina was one of many women who might be a suitable partner for him. This 'the one' business was something invented by Hollywood, anyway.

The longing for her, though, was not something he could rationalise away.

He needed her in his life, no matter what form that took – even if that meant being nice about Will. He grimaced as he thought the name. The man seemed perfect; and like a jealous lover, he'd stalked him with growing hatred. Even the way Will smiled made his stomach churn.

But, Will was the man Gina wanted. And if he was to be part of her life, he had to accept that.

With a deep breath, Sean opened Skype and called Gina. He'd tell her he'd been busy, and she wouldn't know otherwise. She'd likely not even notice he hadn't called her and congratulated her – being so busy with Will. Be nice, remember, he told himself, just in time to plaster a smile on his face to greet Gina with.

'Hi.' Gina gave a small smile, her eyes wary.

Sean gulped. She'd answered! He smiled, hoping he didn't resemble a clown as his cheeks stretched involuntarily. Just hearing her voice, strained though it was, set his heart skittering in his chest. 'Hi.' He caressed her fuller face with his eyes, following the curve of her cheek, and the contentment in her eye. Even though he could tell she was angry, there was a softness to her, and a confidence she hadn't radiated before.

His heart slowed. And it was all down to this Will fellow. He was the one who had made her feel safe. He was the one who was giving her the life she'd always wanted.

For that, he supposed, he should be grateful.

Sean ignored the pang of jealousy in his stomach, and cleared his throat. 'First of all, I'm sorry it's taken so long to call.'

Gina shrugged. 'We've both been busy.'

Touché.

'On that note then, how have you settled in?' He was glad she wasn't angry with him, but it was yet another sign that she was content living without him.

Still, this was what he'd signed up for.

'Good,' Gina gave a wider smile now, making his chest tighten. Being friends with her was going to be harder than he'd expected.

'Have you set up a nursery yet?'

Gina glanced back at the screen. 'Not yet, I'm researching ideas.'

It was the perfect comment to break the ice. Sean laughed, imagining Gina scouring the Internet for pictures, and researching each piece of furniture for safety rating, quality and price. He shook his head and chuckled. How he'd missed her quirks. 'Bet you've got a folder with all your research.'

A pink stain appeared on Gina's cheeks. 'How did you know?'

Sean tapped the side of his nose. 'I have my sources.'

Gina gave a tinkling laugh, and his heart warmed. If this was all he could have, then it was enough, it wouldn't be so bad.

It was better than the alternative, anyway.

Gina hiccupped as she laughed, and waved a hand over her mouth before apologising. 'You can't make me laugh like that now, my body has a mind of its own.'

Sean smiled. *Yes it does,* he thought, hoping his eyes weren't obviously scoping her cleavage. His leg tapped, and he pinched it, hard; before focusing on her hand, which was still in view. Her left hand.

Which was still bare.

'What?' Gina frowned.

'Oh, nothing. Just that . . .' Sean sighed. 'I thought you and Will were engaged.'

It was a stupid thought to voice, but, like the fool he was, he'd done so. But Gina merely shrugged, and smiled into the webcam. 'No. There's no rush. We're happy as we are.'

Sean searched her eyes. She meant it, too. When she was angry, she'd purse her lips and frown, or look away. She never could hide her true feelings.

He should have been grateful he'd escaped so easily, but no. Gina's equanimity only released the jealousy he'd stuffed down. His face twisted into a sneer.

'If I was in Will's position, I would have asked already.' He thought he'd muttered it to himself, but Gina's eyes widened.

'Well, you aren't.'

Sean shook his head. 'No, I mean, it's the right thing to do. Traditionally. From a man's perspective.' He dug his nails into his palms. What was wrong with him? He was supposed to be a diplomat.

Gina narrowed her eyes at him. 'I think I'd better go.'

Sean nodded, staring as Gina's face faded from the screen. He'd been doing so well, until that last idiotic comment. But would she ever speak to him again?

He sighed. Gina was feisty, she would calm down, and, he hoped, accept a grovelling apology.

***

155

Gina stared at the computer screen. *Why do I bother?* She turned up her nose at the screen, before checking that Skype was closed.

Men. They got to act like children, while women took the high road. How many women across the world did the same thing daily, only to burn out eventually and give up on the male species entirely?

Idiots.

She moved to stand up, but stopped halfway. *Why not write about that?* She sat back down, opened a new document, and typed.

Two pages of ideas later, she leaned back and flexed her wrists. Not bad.

Thanks Sean. She felt a momentary pang of guilt at her earlier uncharitable thoughts about him, when her email beeped with a new message.

'Beep.'

A message pinged at the corner of her screen. Sean.

Gina moved the mouse cursor over the blinking message and clicked.

Sorry Gina, I was rude. I only want you to be happy. I hope we can keep up our friendship, but understand if you don't want to. Do spare a thought for the impact of being in the sandpit of a man's mind, though – especially men who aren't super-blessed with suaveness to start with.

Gina's pursed lips eased into a laugh. 'Idiot.' She shook her head. She should give him a second chance. He'd been so kind to her after the carjacking. And she now had everything she'd ever wanted. She could afford to be magnanimous.

Gina clicked reply and began typing a response.

Chapter Thirty Nine

Piece by piece, Gina's new life was settling into place. Her fears about her baby had eased, and now she and Sean were talking again, it seemed that the universe was smiling on her relationship with Will.

All the more reason for her to trust Will more fully. She stood in the hall, biting her lip as she held her new black credit card. *Will told me to buy whatever I wanted; but did he mean it?* Will insisted she keep her own money, but a lifetime of financial independence was a hard habit to break.

She took a deep breath. *I can rely on him.*

'Ready?' Will's head poked around the doorway, his eyes looking from her face to her hands.

'Um, yes, just making sure I have everything.' She shoved the card in her wallet and stood up with a smile, her breath catching in her chest.

Will raised his eyebrows. 'Yes, I did mean what I said. Use the card.' He walked towards her and kissed her on the forehead.

Gina smiled and tilted her mouth towards his for a proper kiss, exhaling with relief. He was getting to know her far too well.

'Have fun.' Phoebe yelled as she and Gina drove away. Will gave her a wink as the car pulled away. Phoebe's daughter Sara perched on his back.

Gina smiled at the image. *He'll look even cuter with a baby carrier.*

'Stop mooning.'

Gina shook her head and smiled. 'Sorry. But he looks so cute with children. He'll be such a great dad.' She sighed.

Phoebe laughed. 'He won't look so hot covered in baby sick.'

Gina smiled, her gaze following the now familiar streetscape of their neighbourhood. Manchester was starting to feel like home.

The car indicators clicked as Phoebe slowed the car down on the high street. Phoebe had a radar for good parking spots, and was unfazed by nudge parking. Gina swallowed. She was yet to attempt it in the new car Will had bought her.

Phoebe zipped the car into the car space and pulled on the handbrake, jolting her thoughts back to the matter at hand: shopping for the new house. She and Will had spent many nights browsing for ideas on Pinterest and in magazines, so she knew their styles were very similar: traditional elegance, simple lines, practical pieces. Things which would one day become heirlooms.

They sauntered over to a nearby shop. 'This lamp is perfect for the baby's room.' Phoebe pointed at a lamp with a white ceramic base painted with rabbits.

'But it's £200!'

'So? Will makes that in ten minutes.'

It was a nice lamp. Will would like it, too. Should she?

Phoebe stiffened beside her. 'Oh, here comes trouble.'

Gina looked up, sniffing at the wave of perfume which hit her nostrils like a powerful punch. She coughed and peered at the tall blonde in extremely tight black jeans and faux fur jacket.

'Oh hiiii, Phoebs.' The woman's brilliant white teeth glimmered in the sunlight.

'Hi,' Phoebe said from the corner of her mouth, raising an eyebrow at Gina, her unspoken gesture of impatience.

The woman waved her hand in the air, clearly hoping they would notice her gaudy yellow diamond ring. 'How is Will?'

The way the woman said Will's name sent a chill

running down Gina's spine. It was playful, almost.

Gina frowned.

'Fantastic. He's married.' Phoebe grinned back at the woman, whose mouth now hung agape.

'Bye.' Phoebe linked her arm in Gina's and propelled her back to the car.

'But he's not married,' she hissed as they put on their seatbelts.

Phoebe put the key in the ignition and shrugged, her eyes on the road. 'Doesn't matter. I wanted to get up the cow.' Phoebe swung the car out into the traffic.

Gina peered at her. 'Who is she?'

Phoebe caught her eye before glancing back at the road. 'That my dear, is the right evil Naomi.'

Gina's jaw fell open. Whatever she'd been expecting, it wasn't that. The woman looked so . . . trashy, and Will was so . . . nice! 'You have got to be kidding. What on earth did he see in her?'

Phoebe laughed. 'Don't fret, love. He's mad about you. Never seen him like this, to be honest.' Phoebe put a hand on her arm before taking it back to the steering wheel.

Gina's chest filled with a warm glow. What she and Will had was unique, for both of them. But it still couldn't erase her curiosity about the woman they'd just encountered. She knew it would be sensible to let the past stay where it belonged, but as the minutes ticked by, her impatience grew.

She turned to Phoebe. 'What happened between them? Clearly they were dating . . . or something.'

Phoebe glanced at her, pursed her lips then looked away. 'It's up to him to tell you, no matter how much I want to.'

'Fair enough.' Gina settled back into her seat with a sigh. How could Will have dated someone like that woman? The way she dressed: so outlandish, where Will was understated. Gina shook her head. *Why am I so concerned about a garish ex? Will is with me now. We're having a baby together.* She frowned. *But then again, how many other women do the same thing?*

'This would be perfect material for *The List*,' Gina muttered, reaching for the phone to email Kara.

'I love that site. My friends and I are hooked on it.'

Gina sat back up in her seat, phone in hand. She'd worried Will and his friends might think she was using her relationship with Will as fodder, so she'd only mentioned she had a book deal to write a Women's Fiction book.

'Well actually, I write it,' she mumbled as she wiped her hands on her top.

Phoebe slammed on the brakes. 'You write *The List*?' said Phoebe, clutching Gina's arm.

'With some help, yes. But you can't tell anyone,' Gina said, eyes widening.

A car tooted behind them, and Phoebe lifted her hand in a wave before accelerating away. 'Why not? You have so much talent. I'd be singing from the rooftops if I were you.' Phoebe glanced over at Gina with a glint in her eye.

'Really?' Little butterflies of excitement fluttered in her stomach. She received emails from women telling her how the list had changed their lives, but it hadn't felt as real as the compliment from Phoebe. She sat up taller in her seat.

'If you write a book, it will be a bestseller. Especially if you have a character like Naomi in it.' She laughed as they pulled up outside a mum and baby shop.

'Does Will know?'

Gina shook her head.

'You're kidding! You are so naughty!' Phoebe landed a playful tap on her arm.

'I was worried he'd think I was using him as a muse.'

She looked up and searched Phoebe's face for any hint of anger.

'I bet he would too. Men think everything is about them.'

Gina laughed and glanced at the store, her stomach clenching with guilt. *Poor Will. I've not been honest with him. What will he think of me now?*

'He'll be thrilled. Just tell him before *I* do.' Phoebe raised her eyebrows in a challenge and grinned.

Chapter Forty

Will set down his paintbrush and surveyed the nursery of their new home. Him, painting. He truly was in luurve, as Phoebe put it. Working on the nursery had nothing to do with trying to put Gina in a good mood before asking for a lad's sailing weekend.

He'd planned to say no to the request at first, given Gina's past history, but he once again felt a pull between his desires and what was best for his relationship. Clearly he was still a work in progress as a family man.

'So have you asked Gina yet?' Hamish asked.

'No. But it should be fine. I was planning to call my mother to stay for the weekend. They can shop and decorate as much as they please.'

Hamish raised his eyebrows. 'Fine? That's optimistic, even for you.'

Will grimaced. 'Let's hope the new nursery smooths the waters.'

He leaned back on his heels and closed one eye. In the dying afternoon light the room still looked bright and inviting. Just the way a baby's room should look.

'I still think we should have used Coconut Cream on the woodwork.' Hamish stood up and stretched his back.

'No, Arctic White was the goods,' said Will. The nursery was almost complete – he had even bought the rocking chair she had liked online. His heart skipped as he imagined her reaction.

'So domestic bliss is agreeing with you then,' Hamish asked, heading to the cooler and pulling out a lager.

'Yes,' Will said, taking the can Hamish handed to him.

'Although the way she lets the toothpaste clog up on the tube drives me crazy, and she leaves lists everywhere. She even writes to-do lists in bed.'

'And you, of course, have no irritating habits whatsoever.' Hamish laughed.

Will rolled his eyes and sipped his lager. *Despite Gina's foibles, I am still crazy about her.* Even work was going well; he'd secured a development deal in Salford Quays he'd wanted for months. It was costing a fortune though, and he'd had to use the new house as collateral to finance the deal –something else he'd neglected to share with Gina. But she didn't need to worry about business in her condition.

He'd said he'd take care of her and the baby, and he would.

'To the women we love,' said Hamish, raising his can.

Will tapped his can against Hamish's. 'To the women we love.'

Gina put on the blindfold as ordered. She'd been waiting for the right time to tell Will about *The List,* but he'd been so excited when she arrived home she couldn't do it. *Plenty of time,* she reasoned.

'If you're trying to have your way with me it's too late,' she giggled as she tottered by Will's side. Will kept his arm around her back, guiding her down the hall. A few steps later, Will removed the blindfold and flicked on the light switch.

The room they'd picked out as the nursery was no longer bare. The walls were pained a crisp white, teamed with a yellow dado, like she'd seen in the magazine she'd been reading recently. A white wooden cot, complete with broderie anglaise bumpers and coverlet, stood by one wall, and a white and yellow gingham checked baby-change stand stood next to it. In the corner was a single armchair on a rocking mechanism. She'd liked it but thought it too expensive – yet here it was. 'It's just what I wanted,' she cried, flinging her arms around him and planting a kiss on his lips. 'I love it.' She grinned at Will, who beamed back at her.

'I'm glad.' Will walked over to her and sat on the arm of the rocker. He kissed the top of her head. 'I told you I would take care of you, and I always will. Both of you.'

Gina's smile faded. *I have to tell him about The List. I can't stand it. He's being so nice, and I'm living a lie.* The fact that she had not told him about her earlier miscarriage was an even bigger secret. She swallowed. That was not a secret he needed to know. *Why worry him unnecessarily?* she reminded herself, before clearing her throat. 'Will, I have to tell you something.' She put her hand on his arm and looked up into his face. Wrinkles formed around his eyes as he frowned at her. 'What? Are you okay?' He glanced down at her belly.

Gina squeezed his arm. 'No, I'm fine, it's not that. It's something else.'

Will nodded. 'Okay.' He gave her a small smile of encouragement.

A lump rose in her throat and she gulped. 'I, um, write a website called *The List*.'

Will laughed. 'Doesn't surprise me. You write lists all the time.'

Gina shook her head. 'Well this list helps women avoid all the mistakes I made with men.'

Will shrugged. 'Why would I be bothered about that? You found me.' Will raised an eyebrow at her, his mouth lifted in a grin.

Gina smiled back. 'I've been so worried. I wasn't sure how you'd take it.' She'd had to run to the ladies multiple times on their shopping trip – ostensibly for morning sickness, but really, it was the thought of losing Will's adoration that had unsettled her stomach. 'She raised her eyebrow

Will laughed and put his arm around her shoulders. 'You worry too much.'

Gina quirked the corner of her mouth. 'I know. I just . . . didn't want you to think badly of me.'

Will lifted her chin to his face. 'I don't. And I won't. No matter what.' His eyes glistened. 'I love you.'

Gina's mouth stretched into a smile. *He loves me! Even with all my quirks and insecurities.*

She searched his face for a hint of deception. Nothing. He meant it – he really did.

Gina placed a gentle, lingering kiss on his lips. 'And I love you.'

The next morning, Gina put her tea cup down on the bedside table with an angry clink, sloshing tea over the lip of the cup and on to the saucer. Had he told her he loved her so she'd agree to this? She glared at him as he stood in the doorway of their ensuite, sheepish expression on his face.

'Sailing is dangerous,' she said, voice raised. Just this morning she'd read about a woman left to care for a baby alone, and then Will said he was leaving for some crazy boys' weekend.

'Gina, it's perfectly safe. You know that, you used to sail in Port Moresby,' he said, moving to the corner of the bed furthest from her.

Gina's jaw stiffened. *Is he mad?* He promised to care for her, yet he was going out on the ocean and leaving her alone. What if something happened to him? She narrowed her eyes at him.

'Fine. If you don't want me to go, I'll stay.' He stood and shrugged.

Gina looked up at him, her anger ebbing away. He

wasn't lying about staying behind – he always scratched his head when he fibbed about eating all the chocolate.

Will sighed and came to her side of the bed. 'I'm sorry, I shouldn't have asked. It's selfish.' He sat beside her.

Gina reached for his hand. 'No. I'm being selfish. It's only one weekend.'

Will stroked the back of her hand with his thumb 'Are you worried because of . . . what happened before?' He raised an eyebrow.

'What do you mean?' Gina's heart pounded. *He can't know! How could he know?*

'I know,' said Will, his eyes locking with hers. 'About the baby you lost.'

Gina froze.

'The doctor let slip something about it when you went to the bathroom. He thought I knew, so I played along. Why didn't you tell me?'

Gina's breath caught in her chest, and her stomach tightened.

He knew.

She should be relieved, shouldn't she? Not panicked that he had found out.

Breathe. The familiar voice came back to her. Sean's voice. He'd taught her how to pay attention to her breath, counting in-breaths, holding, then counting out-breaths, to help her relax when she was overwrought. Gina breathed in through her nostrils, counted to three, and breathed out. She wasn't calm, but the panic had subsided enough that she focused on Will again.

He looked up at her, then back at the duvet, waiting as she composed herself. *Bless the man.*

'I didn't tell you because I was scared – I *am* scared – of losing you, or the baby.' The heart-wrenching loss. The guilt. The fear of never being a mother. She reached for her tea cup, taking an unladylike swig of the remainder of its contents to help wash away the bile in her mouth.

Will took the cup from her, setting it down before easing his arm around her shoulders. 'Gina, it won't happen again. The doctor's certain of that.'

Gina nodded, eyes misting with tears.

'Come here,' said Will, pulling her into a hug.'

Gina closed her eyes and tears slid down her cheeks. The secret was no longer a secret; and the relief, the blessed relief, was overwhelming. In Will's arms, she believed anything. She sniffed, taking a deep breath of his familiar smell, a mix of soap and his favourite cologne. The smell of safety.

'Had you picked out a name?'

Gina opened her eyes and hugged Will more tightly. She'd not said her name since the day she buried her.

It seemed somehow disrespectful to say it, until now.

She swallowed.

'Charlotte.'

Will kissed her on the top of her head. 'Charlotte,' Will repeated. 'It's a beautiful name.' He rubbed her back in a slow circle. 'We could name our baby Charlotte, if we have a girl?'

Gina frowned. She hadn't even thought about doing that, but now she did, her heart resonated with warmth. It would be the ultimate way of honouring her first daughter's memory. A living tribute she could kiss, and hold, and lavish all the affection she'd been unable to give her firstborn. He knew exactly what she needed, before she knew herself.

She sat up, a smile creeping over her face. 'I'd love that.'

Will smiled back and took her hand. 'Maybe that's why we couldn't agree on another name.'

Gina shook her head. 'I'm sorry about earlier. It's just that I worry more when you're not around.' With Will by her side, the shadows of her fears had nowhere to hide, but she had to banish them herself. Will was not some lucky charm to be kept at her side.

'I'll stay, Gina. You and the baby are my priority now.'

Gina shook her head. 'No. I won't live afraid. I want you to go. You're right, everything will be okay.'

Chapter Forty One

Gina stretched and looked at the screen full of words. Will had promised to get Chinese food for dinner if she finished the outline, which had led to another debate. She'd been reluctant to order take out, wanting to save money – which made Will laugh, and say she could spend what she wanted.

But her old habits were still proving hard to break. And while Will might have money now, nothing in life was guaranteed. Will likened her to a squirrel with her saving habits – and in a moment of exasperation she'd told him she was not Naomi. He'd just grinned and kissed her on the top of her head and asked her what take-out she'd like. Was the man ever cross?

Gina gazed over to the television, tempted to turn it on. Not that she'd find comfort there, rather a means to silence the chattering doubt which had woken her in the night: *it's too good to be true. It will all come crashing down, and you'll be alone again.* There was no use talking to Will about it; he'd only tell her to stop worrying.

There was only one person she could talk to about it: Sean. Jen believed she was invincible, and didn't doubt herself. Phoebe was the same. Neither of them would understand her real worry: that without Will by her side, something bad would happen.

Gina glanced at the computer. What would she say? 'Hi, can you tell me that I won't lose my baby?' And what if he was in bed with someone else? If he was, he'd have no interest in playing counsellor to her.

The phone trilled. *Harriet. Oh no.* Gina glanced at the computer screen. At least she almost had an outline. 'Hi Harriet?' Even to her own ear her voice sounded strangled.

'Gina darling. What's wrong?'

Gina cleared her throat. 'Biscuit crumbs. Sorry.' She gave what she hoped was a convincing cough.

'I see. Now I know you're terribly pregnant, but there is a fabulous writing do in Paris coming up, and you should be there.'

Gina gasped. Paris! It might be her last chance to see it for some years, as she had no intention of travelling with a baby. She bit her lip as she looked out the window. But if she went to Paris now, after making such a scene with Will about his trip, she'd be attracting bad karma, surely. And she still couldn't shake the feeling that something might happen when she was without Will.

'Let me talk to Will. I'll call you later, Harriet.'

She ended the call and swirled the mouse on to Skype, clicking on to Sean's name. *Please be there, please be there.*

'Hello, stranger.'

Gina grinned as his picture came on to the screen. Yes, it had been awkward between them since she met Will – but just seeing Sean again reminded her why she'd called. Even on the screen, he exuded calm and caring – and something else. Gina's eyes travelled to his rumpled hair. Had he been in bed with someone?

'Hi. I hope I'm not . . . interrupting anything?'

'Just back from the showers.'

Gina gave a relieved laugh. So he hadn't been in bed with someone. Not that she should care, nor did she want to. She pushed the thought away. 'At least you're taking a shower. I was wondering whether you'd gone all Lawrence of Arabia.' She smiled as she imagined him frowning off into the distance, robed and turbaned. She shook her head.

'Everything okay?' Sean peered at the webcam.

Gina shrugged. 'Fine. But . . . I need your advice on something. And I can't talk to anyone else about it.'

Sean's eyes narrowed. 'Such as?'

'I've been asked to go to Paris for a writing engagement.'

Sean's forehead rose. 'Lucky you. So what's the problem?'

A lump rose in Gina's throat, and she pursed her lips.

Sean sighed. 'Sorry. I'm being a grump. You've caught me pre-coffee.' The sound of a chair scraping on tiles echoed through the speakers. 'You must be doing well to be invited to Paris.'

Gina looked up, giving Sean a genuine smile. 'I suppose.'

'You suppose?' Sean quirked his eyebrow, mouth stretching into a grin.

'Oh stop teasing me.' Her smile widened.

'Can't help it. You are such an easy one to bait! You need to sharpen your skills.'

Gina laughed. 'You can tutor me.' She raised her eyebrows as she waited for his reply. It sounded flirty, now that she thought about it; but hopefully he would consider it lively banter – even if she didn't quite believe that herself.

'Deal. So, when are you going?'

'I'm not sure I want to.'

'It's *Paris*. Send me instead,' he teased.

Gina laughed. 'It's not that, I just, I just . . .'

'You, stuck for words?'

'I'm worried something may happen to the baby,' she said, heart quickening.

'But it's a short trip. And there *are* doctors in Paris.'

'I know, but . . .'

'But what? He hasn't . . .'

Gina shook her head. 'No, no. It's not Will.'

Sean's cheek quirked when she said Will's name. 'It's me. I . . . had a problem when I was younger, and it might affect this pregnancy.' She lowered her eyes, cheeks burning. Surely he would understand what she meant – he was a diplomat, and used to determining the unspoken truth.

'Oh.' Sean cleared his throat. Silence.

The desk blurred as tears filled Gina's eyes. She swallowed past the now painful lump in her throat.

'Oh geez, Gina.' He sighed. 'I'm sorry.' His voice was a whisper.

Gina nodded, eyes still closed. If she looked at Sean's face and saw sympathy, she'd cry harder. 'I didn't mean to make you uncomfortable.'

Sean groaned. 'Don't apologise. You obviously needed to talk to someone. And who better than a diplomat to ease your worries?'

Gina opened her eyes and glanced at the screen. Sean sat, corner of his mouth quirked upwards. 'In a completely innocent sense, of course.'

Gina wiped her cheeks with the back of her hand.

'What has your doctor said about travel?'

Gina sniffled. 'I haven't seen him yet. But the pregnancy has been fine so far.'

Sean nodded. 'Well, it's likely to be fine, then.'

Gina sighed.

'You need to trust him. And yourself. Sometimes you can only do so much, and the rest you need to leave to faith.'

He was right. She'd been looking to Will for strength, when she should have been looking at herself. And faith was not something she had much of. Trust Sean to sense it. 'I hadn't thought of it like that.' Her lip quivered. 'I'm scared, though.'

Sean sighed. 'I would be too.' He gave her a small smile. 'But, you have a little one to be strong for now. And bub wouldn't want you sitting around, hiding now, would he? Or is it she?'

Gina watched Will's fall and lay her fork on to her dinner plate. Obviously this was not going to be an easy conversation. She'd felt so confident after talking to Sean, about herself, the baby, and Will. Now . . .

'Are you serious?'

Gina narrowed her eyes, her earlier feelings of guilt giving way to anger. 'Oh, so you're the only one allowed a trip?'

'That's not what I mean and you know it. Stop being so bloody irrational,' he replied, shaking his head.

'Oh, I'm irrational for wanting to do something for my career. I should sit at home, waiting for the baby to come.' Gina gripped the table, unsure whether to leave the table before she cried.

Will threw his hands in the air. 'I can't win. If I care about you I'm a chauvinist. If I don't I'm a selfish bastard. Can't a man care anymore?' He slumped back in his chair and shook his head with exasperation.

Gina looked at the bags under his eyes and the grey hairs around his temples. Poor man, she was sending him grey. She stood and walked over to Will, kissing the top of his head. 'I'm sorry. I'm being a stroppy cow.'

Will pushed his chair back and pulled her into an embrace. 'Maybe,' he said, tapping her on the nose, 'but you're *my* stroppy cow.'

Gina laughed and reached out to stroke his silky hair, which always soothed her nerves. He leaned his head into her hand, rubbing against it. He opened one eye and smiled. 'Maybe we can find a compromise. If Dr Carlson says you can travel, and I send your luggage ahead, I don't see a problem. Do you?

Gina smiled, her confidence returning. 'No, none at all.'

Chapter Forty Two

'Next stop, Paris Gare du Nord,' the announcer declared.

Gina replayed her last moments with Will as the train slowed. He'd fussed over her before she left, checking her pouch of essential documents, whilst refraining from mentioning her baby brain, bless him.

She removed her eye mask and gazed at her belly, her hands resting on it in what Will called her 'Mama Bear clasp'.

They'll be on the water now. She smiled.

'Stop looking so happy,' Harriet quipped to her side. 'Happy writers don't attract business. Remember to think of something sad tonight.'

Gina grinned. The fact that she was grinning at all was a surprise. Instead of feeling worried on the trip, as she'd expected; she'd savoured the experience. It was yet another piece of her new life falling into place. Zipping to Paris for an event sounded so glamorous, yet it was something she could now do regularly. Better still, she was going to Paris as an author and mum-to-be. Life couldn't get any better.

Harriet wheeled their cases into the aisle and Gina shuffled after her, passengers making way as they caught sight of her bulging belly. Excited or not, she would be glad to reach the hotel and rest on a flat bed. She put her hand on the arch of her back, which now protested at her changed position.

With the help of the man ahead of her she stepped on to the platform, while Harriet stood a few steps away, tickets in hand.

'We might have time for some shopping, if you feel up to it.' Harriet said as Gina reached her.

'Ooh, I'd love that.' *Shopping in Paris. It does get better.*

Her phone rang.

'Will must have heard you say shopping,' said Harriet, arching an eyebrow.

'Ha ha,' Gina said, pulling her phone from her pocket and frowning when she saw Phoebe's number. 'Phoebe, Hi.'

'Gina.' Phoebe's voice shook, sending gooseflesh rippling over Gina's body. She'd thought that something bad would happen to her if they were separated, and now, with sickening clarity, she realised that there was a worse possibility – something might happen to Will.

'*Omega* is missing.'

The platform swirled around her, and the last thing Gina remembered hearing was Harriet calling her name.

When Gina woke it was morning and she lay in a bed with stiff white sheets. She sniffed the air: pine antiseptic. A trolley clattered outside the door.

Definitely a hospital.

She glanced at her belly, but an electronic beep to her right made her look up. She'd seen one of these machines on TV: a heart monitor. The rhythm was steady.

Gina gave a relived sigh, but her chest tightened as she remembered.

Will.

She glanced to her left, where Harriet sat covered in an elegant grey pashmina, an expression of dour stoicism plastered on her sleeping face. Gina attempted to sit up, when Harriet's eyes popped open, and her lips, still bearing long-lasting plum lipstick, parted in a smile.

'Thank goodness.' She swirled the shawl around her

shoulders and stood. 'Will is safe. He's being taken to hospital for routine checks.'

Will was safe. The baby was safe.

Her mind flashed back to their argument. *What if our last words had been cross? I might never have been able to tell him what he means to me.*

She exhaled a long breath. She'd wasted time worrying instead of appreciating. Now she had a second chance, and she wasn't going to waste it with any more negativity. 'When can I go home? I need to see Will.'

'He's still in Cowes, but he'll be here this afternoon.

Gina lifted her eyes heavenward. It was a sign. She'd faced her worst fears, and from now on, she could enjoy her wonderful life with Will.

She closed her eyes. *Thank you,* she prayed. *I will make the most of this second chance, I promise.*

Will sat on the side of the hotel bed, staring out at the sea as tears slid down his cheeks. *I can't remember the last time I cried,* he mused as he stroked the face of his Rolex watch – first clockwise, then anti-clockwise. His thinking gesture, his mother called it.

He had never cared much about dying, but his thoughts while waiting for rescue had been for Gina and their baby. It was his job to look after Gina and their baby, and he'd nearly failed. Worse, he'd let Gina travel alone, when he knew she'd been worried about being without him.

He should have gone with her, and gone sailing another time.

Will wiped his tears with the back of his hand. He'd failed as a father-to-be and as a partner – but he wouldn't make the same mistake again.

He stood up and put on his jacket. He was going to put things right. And first, he was going to Paris to bring Gina and their baby home.

Chapter Forty Three

Will took in a deep breath as the taxi stopped outside the hospital. With its rows of tall arched windows either side of the grand arched drive, he could have been arriving at a castle. He smiled. *A castle – that's where we should marry.*

His smile faded and he patted his jacket pocket, pressing the bulge of the ring box inside. *It's still there.* It wasn't ideal, buying an engagement ring in a hurry; but the Asscher-cut diamond ring had drawn his attention like none of the others had. Like Gina herself.

Will paid the driver and strode to the desk to ask directions, heart thudding. Last time he proposed he'd been greeted by an empty house. He knew Gina was waiting for him – he'd spoken to her as soon as he arrived in Paris – yet the image of an empty hospital room taunted him.

This is different. I know I'm doing the right thing this time.

His heart pounded as the lift climbed towards Gina's floor, becoming louder as he walked the corridor to Gina's room. *This is it, Lockwood. Best foot forward, no matter how you feel.*

He took a deep breath and opened the door, halting at the sight of Gina sleeping with her hands clasped around her belly. The small smile she usually wore when sleeping was replaced by a frown. *That frown is my fault,* he thought with a guilty pang in his stomach. He shut the door behind him and padded over to her side. He'd never take a touch, a word or a look for granted again.

Gina stirred and opened her eyes. 'Will?' She blinked, before reaching her hand out to him.

Will took her hand in his and nodded.

'I'm a bit worse for wear, though.' He touched his forehead with his free hand, flakes of skin coming free as he rubbed.

'I don't care.' Gina pulled her hand away and sat up. 'I'm so happy to see you.'

Will sat on the bed beside her. 'You've no idea how glad *I* am to see you.' He swallowed as tears threatened to fall.

'You scared me,' Gina said, her voice small.

Will gripped Gina's hand. 'I know. And I've learnt my lesson. Forgive me?'

Gina smiled at him. 'I'll think about it,' she said, raising an eyebrow.

Will gave a relieved chuckle. 'I've been thinking, too, and I realised that you're missing something,' he said, producing the box from his pocket. He held it out to her, nodding.

Gina looked at the box, then at Will, her eyes searching his face.

'Open it.'

She eased the lid open and gasped.

'There was something about it,' he started. Gina looked up at him with tear-filled eyes.

'Gina, you and the baby are my world. I won't risk losing you again. Will you be my wife?' He held his breath as Gina looked at the ring, touching it tentatively with her index finger.

'Yes, of course,' she whispered, grinning up at him.

Gina held her breath as Will slipped the sparkling engagement ring on to her finger. *How did I get so lucky? After all those idiots I dated.* She stared at the ring. *But it doesn't matter now.*

She had her baby, and she had Will. A man she couldn't have hoped to meet, let alone be engaged to.

Gina looked up from the ring, her eyes misted with tears. 'Will.' There was so much more to say, but the words wouldn't come. Here was a man who wanted to spend the rest of his life with her, and who had made her happier than she'd ever dreamed of being. Thank you just didn't seem to cover the depth of her gratitude.

Will kissed her. 'I know.'

Gina nodded and wiped away her tears, glad Will was not one to talk much about his feelings. His actions said enough, she thought, glancing at the glinting ring once more.

Engaged. I dreamed about it so often, and now, it's happened. She stared at the ring, her earlier excitement giving way to awe. She was committed now, to Will and the baby. She was responsible for the welfare and happiness of other people.

She pressed her lips together. She'd spent so much time chasing happiness that she hadn't thought about what to do when she found it. Now, she wasn't sure she was prepared for the work that was to come.

Gina sighed, but her breath caught in her chest as a rush of wetness tricked down her thighs. A chill crept over her skin. *It's too early.* She lifted up the sheet, heart lurching as the damp sheets confirmed her fears.

She let the sheet fall and grabbed Will's arm. 'It's time.'

Will stared at her stomach, frowning, and Gina sighed.

'Press the buzzer.' She bit back the other words she wanted to add. He was shocked, like any man would be knowing his baby was arriving weeks early. It wasn't his fault he was standing there looking like a codfish. She probably would too, if the roles were reversed.

'Right.' Will lunged for the buzzer, pressing it long and hard.

***

Will took Gina's ring. 'It will be okay.' He tried to smile, but his lips wobbled, so he pursed them instead. What if something happened to Gina, or the baby? He couldn't lose them now. It would make no sense to be saved, only to lose the very people he'd wanted to live for.

Gina didn't smile back, her attention diverted to the doctors and nurses who now surrounded her. He could only imagine the thoughts running through her mind. She'd worried something would happen to the baby, and she'd been right. It was all his fault.

'They'll be fine, Mr Lockwood.' The doctor nodded at him, then Gina was wheeled away.

Will sighed. I hope so. He looked up at the ceiling. God, I know I've been asking a lot of you these past days, but please, please keep Gina and the baby safe.

'Come, I'll get you some tea.' A small nurse, with the delicate face of a bird, stood by the door.

Will sighed. Drinking tea. So British. A stiff drink would be better.

'Thank you.' He followed the nurse down the corridor, wishing he hadn't convinced Harriet to give them a few hours alone. He could use her strength right now.

Three hours later, Will stroked Gina's forehead as she lay in her hospital bed. He was glad she'd been spared the sight of their baby in a Perspex box, surrounded by people sticking tubes and needles into her. He'd never felt so helpless, standing there, praying she would live.

She looked up at him, her eyes asking him the unspoken question. *The baby?*

He nodded. 'We have a daughter. And she's beautiful.' Will swallowed down his tears. He'd thought better of taking a photograph and showing her, not straight away. He only hoped his words would be enough for Gina, for now at least.

'Thank God,' she mumbled, giving him a weak smile.

Will squeezed her hand. He'd talked to God more these past days than he had in years, and yet, He'd heard him and answered his pleas.

He would make it up to all of them. Gina and the baby would want for nothing. And he'd never ignore Gina's fears again.

Gina frowned at him. 'We have to give her a name.'

Will's lips parted into a smile. This was one piece of news he was genuinely happy to share. 'I already have. Just like we agreed. I named her Charlotte.'

All that glitters

Chapter Forty Four

Does every bride feel this way on her wedding day?

Gina leant on the marble vanity and took one long, deep breath.

At first she'd thought it was just cold feet. Or stress. Having a baby that woke up three times a night didn't help one's nerves. Nor did having dreams that made her wake up, gasping for air, with the sense that the world had shifted underneath her, and that she was once more alone.

Gina strained an ear to determine if Charlotte was settled. *Silence. One blessing, at least.*

She looked up into the mirror, and the perfectly manicured face that looked back at her seemed like that of a stranger.

She had the baby and husband she'd longed for. Charlotte had grown into a healthy baby despite being born prematurely. She should be happy.

What's wrong with me?

'Everything okay in there?' Her mother's anxious face peered around the doorway.

Gina nodded. 'Fine, Mum. Just taking a moment.'

Her mother smiled. 'Okay, but don't be long.'

Gina waited until her mother's footsteps faded, before staring at her reflection in the mirror once more. *It's not just about you anymore, remember.*

She sighed. She'd wanted to talk to Will, but it didn't seem fair to worry him, when she was likely just experiencing pre-wedding jitters. And she couldn't talk to anyone else about it. She'd wanted this life for so long, and now she had it. How could she now say she wasn't sure it was right for her?

They'd think her mad, or ungrateful – and rightly so.

Gina grimaced. For years she'd had a plan, and now she was list-less; in more ways than one.

Will nodded at the random faces smiling at him, glancing left and right for a sign of Gina.

She'd been quieter, but they both had been – neither of them had slept much the last few months.

Yet, today she was more than tired. She'd been subdued through the wedding ceremony, like a woman heading to her doom rather than a happily ever after.

His chest tightened. The nurses had spoken to them about post-natal depression. Had he missed the signs?

Will darted towards the staircase that led to the private rooms reserved for the wedding party. Perhaps Gina was feeding Charlotte before they left.

He took the steps two at a time, arriving at the top of the stairs with a soft plop. He turned towards the private rooms, stopping as he spotted Gina standing in an alcove, gazing out into the garden.

Will paused, watching.

Gina closed her eyes and leant her head back on the wall, her lips moving before she crossed herself.

Will stiffened. What was she praying for?

He wondered whether he should leave when Gina looked straight at him.

It was the briefest glance, but in it, he saw the doubt in her eyes.

'I just needed some quiet.' Gina walked towards him, the dark circles beneath her eyes now showing through her make-up.

Will took her hand. Whatever her doubts, he would be strong for both of us until they passed.

They'd be fine.

Chapter Forty Five

Gina padded out to the kitchen in her pyjamas, Charlotte on her hip.

'Oooh hello, my pet.' Mrs Webster, Charlotte's nanny, had already set the kettle boiling, and was stirring a pot of porridge on the stove. Charlotte held out her arms to Mrs Webster, and kicked her small legs. It was the same every morning, and a routine that made Gina's stomach pang with jealousy. Having a nanny was not what she'd expected, either.

'Just a minute, sweetie.' Mrs Webster turned off the stove and poured the porridge into Charlotte's pink plastic bowl. They'd learnt not to give her any other colour, unless they wanted their ears assaulted by Charlotte's now well-formed lungs.

Gina settled Charlotte into her high-chair, tying a fresh bib around her neck and kissing her on the top of the head.

For the first few months life had been a jumble of feeds, nappies, bottles and bibs. Will had been wonderful, taking over the night feeds and delighting in being a father.

But lately he'd been different. Distant. Moody.

Was he depressed? She couldn't ask him outright. For all his affability, Will was still reserved with his deeper feelings. She sighed. He was a Leo, too, and the horoscope books said to let your Leo man think he is the king. Suggesting he had depression would not be welcomed.

She'd tried writing a list of things to do, facts she knew

and assumptions she was making. In the end she didn't feel any more certain about a way ahead, and watched with helplessness as Will's distance increased.

Gina glanced at the email print out on the kitchen bench. Harriet loved the outline, and was moving forward with her book, yet she hadn't found the right moment to tell Will.

She watched as Mrs Webster fed a spoonful of porridge to Charlotte.

He'd agreed to take her and Charlotte for a drive and a cream tea, to make up for his constant distraction with work.

I'll tell him later today. And maybe it will cheer him out of his blues.

Will leant back in his chair in the study, smiling at the sight of Charlotte gobbling her breakfast. After seeing her so helpless for months in hospital, he savoured anything she did with a relish that bordered on obsession. *Still*, he thought with a chuckle, *being obsessed with your baby isn't a bad way to be.*

His phone beeped and he looked down, groaning when he saw the message. The Salford Quays deal needed more capital, and he'd borrowed more against the house. It was the one thing he'd promised never to do, and the only secret he'd kept from Gina. Every time she smiled at him, his guilt deepened. But if he sold all the units in the development, he would break even, and Gina wouldn't even know about the mortgage. It wouldn't be fair to worry her.

Besides, he'd be in enough trouble when he cancelled their afternoon drive.

He set a smile on his face before padding out to the kitchen.

'Time for a nappy change, young lady.' Mrs Webster

hoisted Charlotte on to her hip. 'Morning, Mr Lockwood.'

Will nodded. 'Good morning.' He waited until Mrs Webster's steps faded. 'I'm sorry, but something's come up. We'll have to do the drive another time.' He gave Gina a peck on the cheek.

Gina frowned. 'But you promised to have today off. You've been working so much I'm starting to feel like a single mother.' She pouted, searching his eyes.

He swallowed. Gina knew something was wrong, but she wouldn't ask him outright. She was biding her time until she found the right way to pry it from him. That was to be expected if one married a lawyer.

Will clenched his jaw. If this meeting went well, there'd be nothing to tell Gina. Will pulled her into a hug. 'I know I've been difficult to live with. You've been a trooper.' He kissed the top of Gina's head. 'It will be over soon, I promise.'

Gina shrugged. 'Okay, well, good luck.'

Will gave her a brief smile. 'Thanks,' he said. *I'll need it.*

'That's fantastic. I knew Harriet would love it.' Phoebe grinned and leaned on the café table, making the cups bounce. Charlotte pointed at them and gurgled. 'So what does Will think?' Phoebe asked.

Gina bit her lip. As much as she wanted to protect Will's pride, she had to confide in someone. 'I haven't told him yet.' She let out a long breath. 'He's never around. And when he is it's as if he isn't truly with me.' She put the coffee cup down as tears welled in her eyes.

'Oh, love.' Phoebe pulled a tissue from her bag and passed it across the table.

'I tell myself I'm worrying too much, but I can't help it.' Gina took the tissue and dabbed at her eyes. 'Something's wrong. And the worst thing is, I don't know what to do.' *Me, the girl who always has a plan.*

Phoebe leant back in her chair, arms folded. 'Men can be moodier than women. Grumpy bastards.'

Gina laughed, her tension easing.

'Best thing I've found? Seduce him. The more sex they get, the better they feel. Then they'll either snap out of it, or they'll be in the mood to tell you what's wrong.'

Gina giggled. 'Surely it's not that simple?'

Phoebe rolled her eyes. 'Most of the time, my duck, it seems to be.'

Will put the note down next to the unopened bottle of champagne and made his way upstairs. He should explain the situation to Gina. She was a lawyer – she would understand better than anyone.

Being honest would at least remove the suspicion between them.

Courage, Lockwood. Don't back down now.

'Gina?'

He searched the room, jumping when he caught a movement in the doorway of their ensuite. His surprise gave way to delight as Gina sashayed out from their ensuite, clad in a silky negligee which clung in all the right places.

Will groaned, his resolution fleeing. This was no time for a speech. How long had it been since they'd made love? His mouth watered.

'Wow.' He walked towards her, leaning down to kiss her perfumed neck.

'Wait,' she murmured, 'I have some news for you.'

Will planted soft kisses up Gina's neck. 'Mmm hmmm.'

'Will . . .'

'I'm listening,' he mumbled as he kissed Gina's chin.

'Harriet loves the outline. They'll take on the book.'

Will met Gina's gaze. It was the first time he'd seen her so happy in months.

And he was going to let her down.

Cad.

He swallowed, forcing himself to smile. 'I am so proud of you.' He kissed her gently on the lips, and she looked up at him, eyes wide.

'Really?'

Will nodded. 'Of course I am.' He traced the lines of her cheekbones with the back of his index finger. So delicate. Like a painting. His painting. He could hardly believe she was his sometimes. 'Now, where were we?'

Chapter Forty Six

The next day, Gina was settling Charlotte into her cot when the doorbell rang. *Will's left his keys again.* She rushed down the stairs, stuffing down an uncharitable flash of anger at the interruption. It was Mrs Webster's day off, the one day she to wallow in her worries without an audience.

Gina stalked to the door, anger increasing with each sock-clad step. The 'baby asleep' sign was up, and Will knew better than to ring the bell. She unlocked the door, mouth set in a frown. 'Will, she's asleep.' Gina flung the door open, ready to launch into a muted verbal tirade; but a large man with far too much aftershave stood on the step. She snapped her mouth closed.

'Babe's asleep, is she?' The man thumped a baseball bat into his fist in steady four-four time.

Gina stepped back to slam the door, but the man stuck the bat between the door and the jamb.

'Tell yer husband that if he doesn't give me the money, the lass'll be sleeping in a tent.' He laughed before turning and walking down the drive.

Gina shuddered as she watched him walk away. They had security gates – people could only get in if they had a remote or were buzzed through from inside. She stumbled into the hall and picked up the phone, hands shaking. 'Damn.' The phone fell on to the floor, and Charlotte let out a wail. 'Coming, baby.' Her voice shook as she picked up the phone and pressed the speed dial button for Will. *Please pick up, please pick up.*

Her breath seemed only to come when Will answered. 'Will, come home, something's happened.'

***

Will settled the duvet over Gina while Charlotte played on the floor beside her. 'Drink this,' he urged, handing her a brandy.

Gina's hands shook as she reached for the glass.

'There'll be more on the duvet than in you – here, let me.' Will held the glass to her lips and she sipped while his mind whirred. He had taken risks before and always come through. *Why had his luck changed now, when he had so much to lose?*

Gina pushed the glass away and glared at him; and his chest tightened as she narrowed her eyes. She was furious – and he deserved her anger. Whatever she said to him, would be nothing compared to the admonitions he'd heaped on himself.

'What the hell is going on?'

Will cleared his throat, his chest tightening even further. 'I needed money for the Salford Quays deal – so I borrowed against the house.'

Gina frowned. 'You what? Without talking to me first?' She shook her head. 'I thought we made decisions together.'

Will's ears burned. Didn't she understand that he was trying to protect her? 'I didn't want you to worry.' He stood, lifting his chin. 'And I *do* know what I am doing.'

Gina gave a low-pitched laugh that sent a chill through Will. 'No, I don't think you do. And what's worse, you put Charlotte and me at risk.'

Will's lips curled in fury. Gina was right, but to hear it said, out loud, was too much for his pride to bear. He knew he should apologise, calm Gina down, but she'd piqued his own fears now.

'And how do you think that feels?' His voice cracked. 'Knowing I put my family in danger?' He glared at her, chest heaving.

Gina narrowed her eyes. 'Why put us at risk in the first place?' She threw off the duvet, picked Charlotte up from the floor and stalked out of the room.

Will stood staring after her, tempted to follow her and press his case. But she'd happily argue with him all night, since she used to argue for a living.

Will snuck to the door and peered out. The light was on downstairs, and the clanging of pots and pans suggested she was taking her anger out on the contents of the fridge. His mouth watered. He hadn't eaten lunch, and by the looks of things, he might not be eating dinner. Whisky. That would at least help him forget his hunger pains until it was safe to grab something from the kitchen.

On any other night he'd go and buy a curry, but he wasn't leaving the house now, not after what happened.

He crept down the stairs and veered left towards his study, closing the door with a soft click. He shook his head. A man should not be creeping around his own house like this. But then again, a smart man did what was necessary when he was in the dog house; and he was justifiably in one now.

But I did it for her. Why can't she see that? He flicked on the light and moved to the desk, unlocking the second drawer and putting the papers on to the desk with a gentle 'plop'. There had to be a way to fix things.

But after an hour of calculating, he slumped back against his chair.

They would have to sell everything. His plans for them were ruined.

Chapter Forty Seven

Gina let the water drain out the plughole, temper rising as the liquid slowly seeped down the drain. In one way, sleeping in separate beds was counterproductive. At least she could have kicked him during the night to take out some of her anger, instead of lying awake, fuming. The fact that he'd lied to her about the money was one thing, but now he dared to ask her to go back to work as a lawyer. The advance on her book was nowhere near enough to keep them housed, clothed and fed.

Her response had been vitriolic. 'No way on God's green earth. Sell your precious car, and the house too,' she'd told him. She had no intention of going back to work as a lawyer to clean up the mess he had made.

The sink now clear of water, Gina pulled out the soap paste and scrubbed it to a gleaming polish. *I shouldn't have married him.*

She scrubbed harder. She'd been so blinded by her image of Will as her knight in shining armour that she'd ignored her intuition – and now she was paying the price.

Gina glanced toward the ceiling where Charlotte's bedroom was. But she had to consider Charlotte. She deserved a stable family.

Gina threw the dishcloth into the sink and put her hands on her hips. Will wasn't the man she'd thought him to be, and that was her fault, not his.

The doorbell rang, interrupting her internal tirade.

'Delivery for Mrs Lockwood,' said a voice from behind a gigantic bunch of red roses.

Gina manoeuvred the bouquet through the hall and sat

it on the kitchen table. She picked up the note with a sigh. *Why do men always think they can fix things with a bunch of flowers?* she thought, as she estimated their cost.

I know I'm not the easiest man to live with. Thank you for loving me, anyway. Will xx

Gina gave a louder sigh and put the flowers in the sink. 'Can't have you dying, given how much you cost.' She pulled the scissors from the hanging rack and snipped the ends of the blooms one by one, her anger easing with each snap of the scissors. As she set aside each stem she breathed deep into her chest, her heart rate calming as she did. Sean had taught her to do this after the carjacking, when he hadn't been telling her stories to help her fall asleep.

Gina smiled. He'd always made her feel so safe, no matter what the circumstances.

She sighed and pulled out the closest chair, flopping into it and glancing at the mantel. The plastic prawn snow globe Sean had given her gleamed in the morning sun.

Warm, salty tears trickled down to her lips, and she brushed them away. There was no point feeling sorry for herself, pining for an imaginary relationship.

Will had wanted to marry her. Sean didn't even want to have a relationship with her.

She stared at the snow globe. She really should get rid of it; no point holding on to a memory.

Gina sighed.

But she couldn't. Not today, anyway.

Will squatted down in front of the gravestone. Clifton Lockwood. Beloved husband and father. If only he was here now to help him. It was the sort of thing you talked to your dad about; rather than your mates.

'I've made a right mess of things, Dad,' he said to the stone as his eyes blurred with tears.

His father would never have made the mistakes he had. His father had worked fourteen-hour days from the time he was fourteen to support his family, taking a job in banking because it paid well. He had worked in that job despite hating it, all so Will and his mother were financially secure. *And I can't even negotiate a business deal.*

He was a failure. Gina thought so, her eyes said it even though she didn't utter the words.

How could he have made such a mess?

But it was done, and he had to rectify it. He had to make Gina and Charlotte feel safe once more.

And maybe, in time, Gina would trust him again.

He wouldn't give up without doing his utmost to win her back.

'Dad, please help me set things straight. I can't lose my family.' He touched the headstone before walking to the car.

Chapter Forty Eight

Will bolted into Gina's bedroom, her screams reverberating in his ears as his heart pounded. Charlotte cried from the cot in the corner of the room, and Will gave a panicked glance toward her. He had to settle Gina first, which would be harder with a baby in his arms. She might be aggressive, too. Will blew Charlotte a kiss. Better to leave her in the cot for now. 'In a minute, precious.'

He darted to Gina's side, sitting on the bed and placing his hands on her shoulders. 'Gina, wake up.'

Gina's eyes flung open, and Will stroked her hair from her face, fighting off the pulses of desire he felt with every touch. Not so long ago, she'd gazed adoringly at him when he'd done this. Would she brush his hand away now? He clenched his jaw. Well, she could push him away if she wanted, but he would still try to look after her. Like he'd promised to.

Gina pulled away from him and darted to the cot as Charlotte's cries reduced to a whimper. 'It's okay. Mummy's sorry she woke you.' Gina scooped Charlotte up from the cot, kissing her on the top of the head before rocking her.

Will stayed by the bedside, his heart slowing to a steady rhythm. 'Do you want to talk about it?'

Gina stared past him at the corner of the room. 'I thought I'd forgotten.'

Will gulped. He'd caused his wife to have nightmares. What kind of husband was he? Sorry wasn't an adequate response, but he could reassure her that she was safe from thugs fronting up on her doorstep. 'He can't hurt you anymore – I told you, the debt is sorted.'

Gina shook her head and leant against Charlotte's. 'It's not that. I was dreaming about the car-jacking.'

Silence. Will exhaled a relieved breath. Gina had finally fallen asleep, while he perched in the wing chair.

Charlotte whimpered, and Will padded over to the cot. He smiled as he gazed at his daughter's sleeping form; one chubby fist raised above her head, the other lying over her satin-edged white cotton blanket. Like mother, like daughter. Gina slept the same way.

Will turned towards the rising and falling duvet where Gina gave a small snore and smiled. Even when she snored she was cute. Would she ever let him call her cute again? He hadn't dared call her darling or baby of late, his tongue halting at the end of his sentences as a result. Being able to lavish affection on her had been so much a part of their connection that its absence caused him physical pain.

He sighed. If all he could do was make her feel safe enough to sleep, then that was enough for now. You had to love people in the way they needed you to. His dad told him that, but until now, didn't truly understand what it meant.

He eased himself back into the chair, eyes focused on Gina's sleeping form. He'd never wanted to look after someone the way he wanted to care for Gina. And it wasn't just because he loved her.

He needed her, when he'd never needed a woman before.

Will clenched his jaw. He wouldn't lose her, no matter how long it took her to forgive him.

***

Gina sat in the doctor's office, clasping and unclasping her fingers as she surveyed his impassive, long face. With his dark, sombre eyes he had the look of a serious donkey. Gina stifled a giggle. An expensive donkey.

She'd had to explain her lack of productivity to Harriet, who had immediately suggested she *see someone.*

It was such a loaded term, and Gina had resisted the idea with a stubborn insistence that she just needed time.

Time passed, however, and the dreams continued.

Will had taken to sleeping in her room now, albeit on a makeshift bed on the floor. The guilt that gnawed at her stomach when she passed it each day, and the growing wanness of Will's face had convinced her she needed help. She'd wanted to punish Will for letting her down, but she was beyond angry now. She wanted her life back; and the only way to find it was to regain her peace.

'Everyone keeps secrets, but some have more impact than others.' The doctor looked at her with his soft brown eyes.

Gina's eyebrows jerked upwards. 'But I'd trusted him to look after me, look after us. That took a lot of faith, and he's let me down.' She looked away. 'I'm not sure I can ever fully trust him again.' They had sold the house and moved into a tiny bungalow. Most of the furniture had been sold too, and the car traded for a cheaper, older version. That didn't bother her greatly, but the changes were visible, tangible reminders of Will's lack of honesty.

And her own.

Will had gotten them into debt but he wasn't the only one who had kept secrets. She had let fear drive her choices, hoping that life would take her in the right direction regardless of the decision she made. Now she was paying the price.

'Do you trust *yourself*, Gina?'

Gooseflesh prickled over Gina's arms. *Bulls-eye.* She

swallowed as she scrambled for something to say, and shrugged instead.

'Why don't you trust yourself?'

He let the silence hang, and Gina squirmed in her leather armchair. 'Because I get it wrong sometimes.' She reached for the glass of water and took a small sip. Each day she stared at the prawn snow globe, wishing for a time in the past; knowing she could never have it. Her heart, however, continued to pine for what she couldn't have; no matter how much she told herself to be happy with what she had.

'Is there a time that stands out for you?'

Gina nodded and bit her lip. 'When I married Will.' Her lips wobbled. 'You see, I think I chose the wrong man.'

Chapter Forty Nine

Two days later, Sean smiled at a street artist playing amidst displays of fake flowers and flashing lights in Trafalgar Square. *Gina would love that. Not that he'd get the chance to show it to her.*

He pursed his lips and turned away from the street theatre.

It wasn't until he'd reneged on his promise to visit Santorini with Ingrid that he'd realised: he wanted to see Gina. He *had* to see her.

But did she want to see him?

He'd booked the flight, ostensibly to spend time at his boss's home in London. His mind had played ping pong the whole trip. *I will, I won't. She will, she won't.* By the time he stepped off the plane, he'd been ready – he would call Gina and ask if she'd meet for coffee. It was harmless enough.

Perhaps not for his heart, though.

The thought of seeing her, happy, with a baby, made his chest tighten with jealousy. He'd been saved from his torment, though, when his boss's wife Harriet had invited him to a cocktail party as her date. He couldn't say no to the boss's wife, even if it put paid to his idea of travelling to Manchester to see Gina.

He kicked at a loose stone on the footpath and squared his shoulders against the drizzling rain.

Gina had taken hold of his heart like a wisteria vine, wrapping herself around it and not letting go.

But she was happily married – and he'd had his chance.

Maybe this change of plan was for the best.

***

Gina walked into Claridge's black-and-white chequered foyer and took a deep breath. *It's just a cocktail party.* She glanced up at the chandelier hanging over the middle of the room. *In a very nice hotel.* Gina surveyed her dress, its blue ruches of plush velvet accentuating her extra curves, and felt a sudden sense of inadequacy. Will liked her post-baby figure, and she'd not considered wearing slimming slips before. Now . . . she grimaced. She felt nothing romantic for Will – there was still too much anger. But she'd wanted to look her best for this event.

Her stomach clenched.

She wanted to look good for others, rather than her husband.

To her left was a gilt mirror hanging over a mantel, and Gina veered towards it to check her make-up. The dark circles under her eyes were dulled by concealer, but still visible. Her grey hairs were also covered, thanks to the hasty home hair dye job she'd done the other night. Only the grim-set mouth suggested she was not as youthful as she appeared. She shrugged. Harriet would be grateful she was here at all. Her looks didn't matter.

'Good enough.' Gina turned to walk away.

'That's a stingy assessment.'

She froze. *There was something about that voice. Something familiar.*

Was it?

She turned, heart pounding, before locking eyes with Sean.

Gina's breath caught in her chest as a slow smile spread across his face.

Her heart slowed, and the tension in her stomach eased as her own lips parted in a smile, too.

The old sense of being home, and safe, returned.

Gina looked down and swallowed, hard. *Oh Lord, help me. What do I do now?*

'There you are!' Harriet bounded over, red hair swishing.

Gina gave a quick glance heavenward. *Thank you.* She shrugged at Sean before Harriet towed her away.

'Now this man on my right with the pink bowtie is Gavin Oliver, head of public relations for our authors. Just watch his hands when you stand next to him,' Harriet whispered. Gina nodded, a wave of gratitude washing over her as Harriet fired titbits of gossip at her. She glanced out of the corner of her eye for Sean, but was twirled away from the door. 'Oh, and this lady to my left with no eyebrows is Gabby Fisher, not invited but just turned up, regardless. Defected to our rival publisher Connor & Jacobs last month. She's still gathering information through her husband, who works for us as head of accounts,' she whispered. 'Gabby,' Harriet said as she whirled Gina up to meet her.

It felt like three hours but it was only thirty minutes before she extracted herself with the excuse of using the ladies. With a furtive look behind her, Gina turned for the lobby instead of the bathrooms, zooming towards an empty huddle of wing chairs in a darkened corner. The perfect place to collect her thoughts, and decide what to do about Sean.

Her clutch landed on the coffee table with a soft 'plonk' as she sat down. 'Ahhh.' Gina breathed out and leaned back into the soft padded fabric before kicking off her shoes, closing her eyes as she wriggled her newly-freed toes.

'A bit early for that, Cinderella.'

Gina's eyes flickered open to see Sean's head peeping up over the opposite wing chair.

'What are you doing here?' She frowned.

Sean gave her a small smile, before taking the chair beside hers. 'Harriet is my boss's wife. I'm here as her handbag, I guess you'd say.' He laughed. His face bore more wrinkles around the eyes, but they still danced with the mischief of a young boy.

Gina smiled, raising an eyebrow at the smattering of grey at his temples. 'You're looking very distinguished with the salt and pepper effect there.' Even she could hear the flirty undertone in her voice, but she stuffed down the rising sense of danger within her.

They were only talking. She wasn't doing anything wrong.

'That's your fault.' He searched her eyes, before raking his gaze over her figure.

Gina swallowed as a surge of desire ran through her. *I have no longing for Will, but I see Sean and bam! I'm thinking about getting a room upstairs.* She looked at the piping on her chair, picking at it and hoping her cheeks were not bright red.

Sean reached out and put his hand on hers. 'That is very annoying.'

Gina gulped. He was so close, and smelt so good. 'Nervous habit,' she stammered.

He said nothing, but ran his fingers over her long delicate fingers, stopping at her rings. They both stared at them.

'So he's not short of a quid I see,' he said dryly.

'I'm lucky to still have these,' she whispered as tears stuck in her throat.

Sean sighed, then squeezed her hands. 'Let's go for a walk, hey?'

The pub they chose was tucked away in a side-street, its carpet worn, and the atmosphere hazy. But it emanated a sense of comfort, like an old pair of slippers. Neither of them had considered the fancier bars they'd passed—and they'd both veered to this one when they saw it.

Will would have stopped at the fanciest bar. But with Sean, she didn't need to say anything.

Gina took another sip of her wine. 'And ever since the man came to the house, I've had nightmares about the carjacking.' She took another sip, fiddling with the stem of her glass. 'The worst of it was, I couldn't shake the fear during the day. I was taking Charlotte to the toilet with me in case something happened to her.'

Sean leaned across the table. 'Is there something I can do?'

Gina stiffened as her thoughts returned to her and Sean in a room at Claridges. She swallowed. 'No, but thanks.' She smiled, hoping it looked genuine. 'But enough about me. What have you been doing with yourself?'

Sean shrugged. 'An endless stream of cocktail parties and functions, it seems. Nothing as exciting as Moresby.' He smiled. 'Which is why I've volunteered to go to back to Afghanistan.'

Gina froze. 'When?' Her voice was almost a squeak.

'Next month.' Sean's smile faded. 'Don't worry; I'll be fine.' He reached out across the table and took her hand again.

Sweat beaded on Gina's palm, and gritted her teeth. *I don't know if I can stand much more of this.*

They stayed silent, hands locked, neither one letting go.

'I almost forgot,' Sean said eventually. He eased his grip on her hands and reached into his jacket pocket, before handing her an envelope. 'I was planning to mail this to you.'

She took the small package, and ripped open the top of the envelope. Photos tumbled out.

'I thought you might find this useful for your writing.'

Gina flicked through the pile. There were dozens of

photos of young children playing and going about their daily life in Afghanistan. Women doing their chores. Men tending their fields.

'There's a young Afghani photographer who's making a name for herself. I've been buying photos from her every week.'

Gina was drawn in by the candid images. They captured people lost in their thoughts, unconcerned about whether they were being observed. Just the sort of people watching she loved.

'I thought it might inspire the writer in you.'

And I thought he wanted to forget me. But he was thinking of me, even in a war zone.

Sean took another sip of the whisky his boss, Mitchell, had left in his room. It was his best; a sign of Mitchell's gratitude that Sean had taken his place at the do with Harriet tonight. Not that it had been a chore.

He swirled the amber liquid around the glass, hoping it might soothe the ever-present whirl of competing emotions he'd been wrestling with since seeing Gina. For months he'd fantasised that she would pine for him and regret her choice. Then he'd tried being angry with her. But he still could not bring himself to throw out his photos of her.

And now she was back in his life.

When he'd told her he was going back to Afghanistan, the look of undisguised anguish on her face made his heart squeeze like a vice.

She cared all right; like he cared for her.

He sighed. It should have been him looking after Gina – and if he hadn't left Port Moresby after the carjacking, it could have been.

Chapter Fifty

Gina rested her head against Sean's shoulder, the afternoon light streaming in through the sheer curtains of the hotel room. Gina couldn't remember how long they'd been sitting this way, perched between a future together, and a future apart. The bed, still made, beckoned temptingly.

It was always the same room. Modern; but comfortable. Apart from the bed, the room was empty. Yet, it felt warm – like everything that mattered was in that room with them.

'My next posting will be in London,' Sean said in a low voice.

Gina sat up. 'But you wanted Port Moresby.' She frowned.

Sean took her hands in his.

'I did – but things have changed. I want to be with you.'

'But I'm with Will.'

Sean lifted her chin up so her eyes met his. 'I know, my timing is rotten. But if I say nothing now I will never forgive myself. If you never want to see me again I understand. But I had to tell you before I left.'

In her dream Gina had shaken her head and bit her lip. Sean had wiped away her tears with his thumb, cupping her face in his hands before pulling her to him for a kiss.

'Sean, this isn't right.' Gina pulled away.

'How can it not be right? I love you and want to be with you. Don't you feel the same way?' Sean clasped her hand in his and stroked her skin with his thumb.

Dream Gina had looked down at his hand stroking hers. 'I have to think of Charlotte.'

'I will love Charlotte as if she is my own.' Sean moved towards her and held her arms, but she looked down at the floor to avoid his gaze. 'You know that. You just want a reason to take the easy way out.'

'This is not the easy way out,' Gina sobbed. 'It's the right thing to do.'

'It's the gutless thing to do,' Sean had said before stalking out the door.

Yet another dream. A dream about the man she couldn't have. Shouldn't have.

But wanted, anyway.

They'd agreed to meet up once more before he left for Afghanistan. *As friends*, Gina reminded herself.

Her mind and heart had been fighting each other all the way down on the train. *How can you know you love him? You thought you loved Will, and you got that wrong.* Over and over her mind had taunted her, reminding her of all the mistakes she'd made; yet her heart rallied every time. *You know you love him. You know he's the one for you. It will turn out okay if you follow me.*

By the time she reached London, she was no clearer about what she would do when she saw him.

Gina hurried through the drizzle, not bothering with an umbrella. *Maybe if I look bedraggled, he won't be interested,* she thought, losing herself in the London crush outside the station. *Then the decision will be made for me.*

Her will strengthened as she walked. *Even if he does want me, I just have to say no. For Charlotte's sake.* She grimaced as she pictured Charlotte sitting on Will's knee while he read her a story, her eager face reaching up to stroke his cheek.

I can't do it to them. It will break their hearts.

She pondered what to say as she wound her way to the hotel, rejecting every suggestion that came to mind.

Gina let out a deep sigh.

No matter what she did, someone would be hurt.

When she married Will, she'd taken on his happiness too, and they were both responsible for Charlotte's.

That wasn't her only concern. If she walked away now, when things were bad, would she regret it later? If she left Will, she'd have to explain it to Charlotte one day – and telling her she left her dad because she loved someone else just didn't seem right.

She reached the hotel and veered towards the wall. *You can do this. You have to do this.*

Gina closed her eyes, breathed deep into her belly, then walked towards the hotel's revolving glass doors – until a movement caught her eye.

It was the flick of a wrist as a man straightened his paper.

That watch. Sean's watch.

She stood, staring as the crowd moved around her. *One last look before I end it,* she thought, tears springing to her eyes.

Then the paper lowered, and Sean's eyes locked with hers.

Sean stared back at Gina's flushed face, glancing briefly at her heaving chest, then back up to the frown now wrinkling her forehead. She always looked like she was solving a deep problem, he thought with a smile. It was one of the things he loved most about her – her passion for everything-including, it seemed, for him.

She raised her hand in a wave, before running her hand through her hair, the way she always did when she was about to have a serious talk with someone.

Sean folded his paper and placed it on to the glass side

table, watching as Gina made her way over to him. She'd tried to hide her feelings – diverting her gaze, keeping a physical distance – but when their eyes met, there was no mistaking the desire and fear that mingled in hers.

A gentleman would respect her hesitation, and her marriage vows – yet he knew he was about to behave like a cad. He had no intention of respecting her marriage. How could he, when he knew, finally, that Gina was the love of his life? If they followed their hearts, everything would work out.

He stood up as she came towards him. 'Hi,' Gina said, giving him a shy smile.

'Hi.' Sean placed a gentle kiss on her cheek, his lips tingling as they touched her skin. He drew away slowly, noticing Gina's sharp intake of breath as he did. Now was the time. No long speeches, just show her how he felt. Talking could come later. 'Come up for a minute. I forgot something.'

Gina glanced up, eyes flickering between his. She knew he was lying, he never forgot anything. But she nodded her agreement anyway.

Sean's heart pounded as he took Gina's hand and led her to the lift. In moments he'd be running his hands over her – all of her. The air hung heavy with anticipation as they stared at each other, breathing long, slow breaths. Finally, the lift pinged its way to Sean's floor, and the doors opened.

Sean led her to the room in silence. There were no words to say to convey how he felt, and if there were, they'd come out wrong, anyway. He could barely step one foot in front of the other his heart was being so loud. His hands fumbled for the plastic key in his back pocket, and he swiped it, before motioning Gina through, and letting the card fall to the floor.

He had her in his arms in an instant, pushing her up

against the wall; his senses afire as their lips met.

Whether this was right or wrong, he didn't care.

She was here, and she would be his.

Gina pressed herself into Sean's arms, losing herself in his spicy cologne and the feel of his hands against her back as he pulled up her blouse. She'd dreamed of this moment so many times she'd almost tasted his kisses and felt his skin on hers.

But now, as Sean pulled her shirt out from her jeans, guilt mingled with her desire.

If she slept with Sean, it would lead to more lies, and heartbreak. And if she split from Will, she might not be allowed to remain in the country.

She couldn't leave Charlotte, no matter the cost to her own happiness.

She put her hand on Sean's chest, and he lifted his lips from her neck.

'I can't.'

Sean stepped back, panting, his jaw working as he caught his breath.

'I love you,' he said levelly, his hazel eyes pleading with hers.

'I know,' she said, turning away from his gaze. It was bad enough she was breaking her own heart; she couldn't watch as she broke his, too.

Gina tucked her blouse in before looking back up at Sean. 'But it's not just about us anymore. I have to think of Charlotte.'

Sean put his hands on her arms. 'I'll look after Charlotte as if she's my own.

'I know you would.' She bit her lip. 'But I can't risk losing her by leaving him.'

She shook her head, and Sean sighed, taking his hands from her arms.

'What a bloody mess,' he groaned, leaning his head back and covering his face with his hands. He stood like that for a moment, before removing his hands and shaking his head. 'I didn't think of that.'

'Neither did I.' Gina sniffed, and Sean glanced at her with a frown.

'Gina, don't feel guilty. It was my fault.'

Gina looked up at him, eyes now streaming with tears. He really was like a knight, gallant to the last. And this would be the last time she would see him. They couldn't be friends, not after this.

Their eyes met, and she knew as she looked into his that she didn't need to say any more. She didn't need to tell him she loved him, or that she would leave Will if it wasn't for Charlotte. And she knew he was berating himself for not being brave when he had the chance, as she was.

Gina reached up and stroked his cheek, her hand trembling. 'I shouldn't have come. I'm sorry,' she mumbled before walking out the door.

Chapter Fifty One

Gina sat on Elly's couch, her stomach leaden with guilt. Coming to Elly's for Will's birthday had seemed like a good idea; a third party to make the tension less noticeable. But the longer she sat, the more concerned she grew. Could she tell that she'd almost cheated on her son?

A carriage clock ticked on a side-table, as if assessing her guilt. Tick, guilty; tock, guilty. Gina shook her head and glanced out the window at the empty gravel drive. How much longer would Will be? For the first time in months, she was eager to see him.

Elly pointed to the photo of Will's father. 'Will is so much like him, always looking on the bright side.' She paused, mouth turning into a frown. 'Well, he used to.'

Gina's stomach churned. Was Elly blaming her for Will's changed mood? Gina bit her lip.

'I'm sorry.' Elly reached over and clasped her hand. 'It's not you, *ma chere.*' Her eyes clouded. 'He seems . . . unsure of himself. I've only seen him look that way when his father died.'

Gina sat still, not sure what to do. She was sure Will hadn't said more than was necessary about their financial troubles. But did she know about their separate bedrooms?

Charlotte's rattle rolled away, and she whimpered. *Thank goodness for small mercies*, Gina thought, lunging from her chair to pick up the rattle.

The sound of footsteps crunching on the gravel driveway outside broke the silence. No money for two cars now; Will would have had to walk from the station for the first time in years. *Serves him right*, she thought, before remonstrating with herself.

'Ah, here he is.' Elly beamed at her.

Gina picked Charlotte up from the rug and cast a longing look towards the bottle of wine on the table. It was going to be a long night.

Will's shoulders sagged as he looked at the pristine black door of his childhood home. If he could have one birthday wish come true, it would be to have his family back like it used to be. He didn't care about the house or the car. Those things could be bought. People couldn't. Not the ones that mattered, anyway.

It was like a slow form of torture watching his wife slipping away from him, and being powerless to stop it. He knew not to press her: Gina was as stubborn as a goat, especially when she was upset. It fought against every instinct he had not to use his strength to win her back, but this was a subtle, long-term battle. And the thought of losing made his stomach churn.

But she's still here, he reminded himself. *Give it time.*

Will stood on the stoop, taking a last reinforcing breath before the night ahead, when his mother opened the door.

He smiled despite himself. *At least someone's always happy to see me.*

'Happy birthday, *mon cher,'* his mother said, kissing his cheek and squeezing him into a hug.

'Thanks, Mum.' He rested his chin on her shoulder, holding on to her a little longer than usual. She may have been small, but his mother's strength gave him courage.

The smell of roast chicken wafted down the hall, and his mouth watered. Mum's roast chicken also gave him strength.

Gina walked up behind his mother and gave him a tight smile. 'Sorry, she couldn't wait.' She looked down at Charlotte, who was holding a small gift in her hands.

Elly ushered them into the lounge and they sat, Gina bringing Charlotte over and placing her on Will's lap. Their fingers touched, and he looked up at her, hoping to catch her eye, but she walked away and sat on the opposite sofa.

Will tried not to frown. 'What have you got here, sweetheart?' He ripped the wrapping off quickly; passing it to Charlotte's outstretched fingers before coughing at the sight of the familiar box. His Rolex watch. His father had bought it for his twenty-first birthday; but he had sold it soon after they moved out of their house, despite Gina's protests. There was no room for sentimentality in the face of bankruptcy.

Elly gasped.

'Gina, you shouldn't have,' he whispered.

'I know how much it meant to you.' Gina looked down at the floor.

Will shook his head and looked back at the watch. She still cared – else she'd have bought him something less meaningful.

He smiled. It was going to be a good birthday after all.

Chapter Fifty Two

The next day, Gina gulped down another glass of water and winced at the sunlight streaming in through the kitchen window. At least it was Mrs Webster's day off, and she could nurse her hangover in private.

She turned off the baby bottle steriliser at the power point and headed to the utility room, grateful for the pile of washing that greeted her. It seemed that the smaller the person, the more mess they made. Gina sorted through the pile, one ear listening to the children's program Charlotte was watching, the rest of her mind tormented with guilt. The strain of pretending she and Will were okay had been far more draining than the wine she'd drunk. She only hoped she'd done a good enough acting job so as not to concern Elly.

If she could force her heart to be happy with Will again, she would. He had given her a beautiful daughter, and a mother-in-law she loved as she did her own mother.

It will take time, she reasoned. *Be patient.*

Gina threw in a load of colours and padded back to the lounge, ready to indulge in a morning of coffee and CBeebies, when she spotted Charlotte with the remote.

'Igg-ool.'

Gina glanced at the clock. 'Clever girl, it's *Iggle Piggle* time.' She was about to change the channel when a news flash came on to the screen.

'We have just received breaking news of an attack on Australian officials in Afghanistan. We are aware of one allied civilian casualty, others have been kidnapped. More news as it comes to hand.'

The remote fell to the floor.

Gina blinked, the room coming into bleary view. 'No. No!' She wanted to scream, but Charlotte was already scrunching up her face in sympathy. A screaming baby would not help matters.

She leant down and scooped her up, her mind doing frantic cartwheels. *It may not be him, there are plenty of foreigners in Afghanistan.* But the harder her mind tried to convince her otherwise, the heavier the lead weight in her stomach became.

If you find Sean, I'll be a good wife to Will no matter how I feel, she prayed. *I promise, on the life of my child.*

Gina sat on to the sofa before changing the channel to Charlotte's show and putting her on to the floor, tears streaming down her cheeks. If she hadn't said no that day, he might not have gone back to be kidnapped. She opened her mouth, gulping in a lungful of air, trying to calm herself as her heart and head pounded. *It's my fault,* she thought, glancing heavenward. *So don't punish Sean. Please.*

Will flicked on the lights and surveyed the toys strewn over the floor, the messy cooker and uncleared plates. The house was usually spotless. 'Gina?' he yelled, striding over the tiles.

Gina peered up over the sofa. 'In here.'

Will took in the red eyes and puffy cheeks and ran the last few steps to her, his heart racing.

He sat beside her and noted the pile of scrunched up tissues, and the empty yoghurt packets she'd obviously fed Charlotte, but hadn't discarded. She hated mess. How long had she been like this?

'Are you okay?' Will peered at her, trying to catch her eyes, but she looked down at the crumpled tissue in her hands and nodded.

'I'm okay,' she said, voice shaking, 'but a friend of mine

is in Tarin Kowt.' She stopped, taking in a deep breath. 'And . . . I don't know . . . if he's alive . . . or dead.'

Will frowned. He? The way she said it left no doubt there was more to it than friendship. She was a terrible liar at the best of times, let alone when she was upset.

He clenched his jaw. He would not blame Gina for looking elsewhere, if he was honest, but his pride wasn't interested in honesty. Gina was his wife, and this man had upset her. It sounded irrational, he knew, being angry at the guy, whomever he was, for being kidnapped. He took in a deep breath. But Gina needed him, and he wouldn't improve things between them by acting jealous.

'I'm sorry about your friend – and that things have been so awful lately.' Will put his arm around Gina's shoulder, and she leant her head on to it, before curling herself up into a ball beside him. Her shoulders shook as she began crying again, and he tightened his arm around her, the familiar smell of her shampoo catching in his throat.

'So am I.' Her low voice was so defeated, so desolate, he pulled her into a hug, rocking her as she cried.

Whoever he is, he won't ruin our family, Will thought, stroking Gina's hair. His jaw tensed once more. *We'll get through this, together.*

Chapter Fifty Three

Gina looked at the photos on the mantelpiece and smiled. Their wedding day, Charlotte's first steps, and their first holiday as a family. The knowledge she had a loving husband, a daughter and a home should have been enough to convince her she was doing the right thing, but she could not break free from the spell of the man who haunted her.

But I will. I have no choice.

Sean was still missing, despite months of fervent government-led negotiations. There wasn't even certainty the hostages were still alive. Gina had become adept at pretending she had accepted the fact to everyone else, and now all she had to do was trick herself.

Gina turned back to the mantelpiece and her eyes rested on the gaudy plastic prawn which she couldn't bear to remove. It looked so out of place amongst the other pieces, but to her, it was still precious. She gingerly picked it up and tipped it upside down, watching as the silvery pieces of glitter traced to the bottom of the fake ocean scene.

Having Sean as a friend was the bargain she had made, but now she didn't even have that. She'd been swindled.

She'd railed at God, demanding to know why he had taken Sean when she'd agreed to stay with Will. She'd even told God she would fight him if he dared to try to take Will or Charlotte away from her. But He was silent.

And after months of fuming, she was tired. Being angry all the time had distanced her from Charlotte and Will, and affected her writing. Harriet had told her to take some time out after she submitted a partial draft, and

Gina knew it was because what she'd written was an angry rant about love. Her anger was poisoning her life, and if she let it continue, she would lose the life she'd sacrificed Sean for.

Gina took the prawn to the bin, her heart racing. It was time to say goodbye.

She stood by the bin, ready to lift the lid, and looked down at the prawn still in her hand. 'I love you, Sean,' she whispered.

Footsteps sounded behind her, and she tensed.

'Who's Sean?' Will growled.

Gina kept her back to him, heart pounding in her ears. Tension filled the air, so she reached out and placed the snow globe on a nearby bench, a second before Will grabbed her arms and turned her to him.

'*Who the fuck is he?*' Will yelled, his eyes wild.

Gina swallowed. She knew instinctively that her best response was to stay calm, which was far easier to do now that she'd made the decision to let Sean go. Weeks ago she would have goaded Will to assuage her own guilt and anger; but now, she just wanted peace.

'What does it matter, Will?' Gina whispered, prying Will's hands from her arm.

Will shook his head. 'Is Sean the guy who's been kidnapped?' A red stain crept up his neck, and the cords of his neck bulged.

Gina looked into Will's eyes. They pleaded with her to say no, this other man meant nothing to her; that he was the only man she loved.

She sighed. Will deserved better than to have his heart broken over a man who would never physically come between them.

'No.' She pursed her lips. 'Now get out of my way.' She darted around him, only letting her tears fall when she'd left the room.

***

Will paced the floor, fists curling and uncurling in unspoken rage. Gina was lying, but why did it matter? She was still with him, if he could call it that. He picked up the snow globe and raised his hand, ready to throw it at the wall. *Break it and she'll only become more distant.* He lowered his hand and put the globe back on the bench, then walked over to the drinks cupboard. He *had* lost her, even if this Sean wasn't in the country to take her from him. He picked up the crystal whisky decanter and poured himself a glass before gulping it down, then poured another straight away and downed that, too.

He'd suspected she was in love with this man who'd been kidnapped, but hoped he'd been wrong. Now, having it confirmed made him want to retch, despite the liquid warmth that now seeped into his belly.

Had Gina been lying all along? He put the glass down and rested his hands on the walnut surface of the cupboard, his eye catching the reflection from their silver-framed wedding photo. She hadn't been sure on their wedding day, though he was sure she loved him. He'd felt that, at least, even if she had been a bit shaky.

His eyes travelled to the other family photos beside it – Charlotte's first visit to a Christmas markets, her rosebud mouth pouting. A photo of Charlotte with Gina's lipstick smeared all over her mouth. Gina and Will, smiling at each other at Hamish and Phoebe's party.

No. She did love me. So what was it about this Sean that made her change her mind?

Will sighed and shook his head. Gina was right. What did it matter? He'd drive himself mad going on like this. Besides, he would win her back; he was making money again, and once he showed her he was looking after her like he'd promised, things would get back to normal.

Perhaps even better than normal.

He looked back at the shelves of photos, his heart leaping.

And maybe one day we'll have other baby photos on the mantel, too.

Chapter Fifty Four

Gina rolled the coffee cup around her hand, anything to fill the loaded silence of her messy kitchen. This last week she'd struggled to do the chores, not that Will had complained. He'd made pasta with ready-made sauce for dinner each night and planned to try a tuna bake tonight. She glanced down at her nails. They could use a good manicure, but she didn't even have the energy to file them.

I thought I'd feel better, letting go of the anger, she mused. But Dr Donkey said that grief could take years to recover from.

Years of feeling like this, she thought with a sigh.

'How are you, duck?' Phoebe peered at Gina, pushing her face into her view.

Gina pursed her lips. 'I am not some circus curiosity.' She frowned, hoping Phoebe might leave her in peace.

'With that complexion I beg to differ.'

Gina looked at her now, eyebrows raised. Clearly Phoebe wanted to pique her into conversation. Well, it was the least she could do, after Phoebe had put up with her moping. 'Thanks.'

'I know what you need. A nice day out at the day spa?'

Gina sat back in her chair. 'You've already booked, haven't you?'

'Maybe,' Phoebe said, rolling her eyes upwards as if trying to remember.

Gina sighed. She had to do something to improve her mood. What example was she setting for Charlotte? And she had to do better than this for Will.

She looked over at the oven, where the ready-mix cake Will had baked was rising. He'd promised Charlotte a cake and had made it without even calling his mother for help.

'I guess so. Will is here with Charlotte . . .' Gina replied.

'Will. Get her coat, quick,' Phoebe yelled, as Will flung open the kitchen door, coat in hand, jiggling it in anticipation of Gina putting it on.

Gina walked over and let Will help her into the coat, remembering to smile when he kissed her on the cheek. 'Thank you.'

He grinned at her. 'Have fun. We'll have dinner ready when you get home,' he said, eyes shining.

'Great.' She smiled back with a heavy heart. 'I can't wait to try it.'

Will groaned. Sleeping in a wing chair was a stupid thing to do, but Gina had been so low all day he'd been scared to leave her. The day spa idea had seemed like a good way to get her interested in the rest of the world again, but Phoebe said she'd been like a statue the whole time. She'd barely touched her food, either.

His instincts told him she was trying, and his heart ached at the struggle he saw within her. It had led him to the realisation that there was another way.

Gina loved this other man; or so she thought. But while he was a ghost, she didn't know for sure. If he helped her find him, she would at least have the chance to make a choice, and stop being a ghost herself.

Gina stirred and switched on the light, wincing. 'What are you doing here?'

Will stood up and redirected the lamp towards the corner of the room, casting it in a comforting glow.

'I was worried about you. Wanted to make sure you slept well,' he said, shrugging and sitting on the empty side of the bed.

Gina sighed and wriggled into a sitting position. 'Will, I've been unfair to you.'

Will's mouth fell open, and his stomach clenched. *What was she going to say? That she'd slept with the man? Or worse?*

Gina looked down at her hands and he watched, his breath caught in his chest. 'I wanted a family,' she said, looking up at him 'and when I met you, it all happened so quickly.'

Will sighed. That was a relief. He reached out, resisting the temptation to pull her into a bear hug, and put his hand over hers instead.

Now was the time to tell her he'd help her find this other man, tell her he'd set her free if that's what she wanted.

But as he looked at her sagged shoulders and drawn face, his mouth wouldn't form the words. As noble as the sentiment had been, when it came to it, he couldn't help Gina find someone else. He loved her too much to let her go, selfish though it seemed.

He cleared his throat. 'Enough of that. It doesn't matter. What matters is what is here, now. You, me and Charlotte.' He reached over and put his forefinger under her chin, lifting it gently to face his. Although she averted her gaze, her chin trembled under his finger. 'I said I'd look after you, Gina, and I will.'

Gina lifted her hand and covered his.

'I know you will.' She looked up at him now with tired but determined eyes.

He hadn't seen that look for such a long time.

There was hope.

Will smiled, his heart warming. 'I thought you might have a restless night. So I bought a book in case you woke. If you like I can read it to you.'

Gina gave him a small but genuine smile, and his own

smile broadened as she did. 'Really? Which one?'

'*Persuasion.* I know it's your favourite.'

She peered at him, and he wondered whether she would kiss him. Instead, she nodded.

'Thank you.' She eased back on to the pillows, her face turned towards him.

Will swallowed the lump that had formed in his throat. The kiss would come.

'Sir Walter Elliot, of Kellynch Hall, in Somersetshire, was a man who, for his own amusement, never took up any book but the Baronetage.'

Chapter Fifty Five

One year later

'Will,' yelled Gina. 'You promised to look after Charlotte so I could write, remember?'

Will thumped downstairs, hiding his smile as he turned the corner towards their poky rental kitchen. There'd be no chipped tiles in their new house, and no more broken appliances, either. He glanced towards the casserole on the range, which emitted comforting smells of rosemary and chicken. Things were almost back to normal.

After months of hard work, and a good dose of luck, they were debt free. Before he told Gina though, he needed to fetch the eternity ring he'd put on hold. She deserved that and more for staying with him through it all. And she would have it, from him at least. Whoever he was had not returned, and slowly, they had made their way back to each other. It had been more difficult than he'd imagined, loving his wife while she wasn't truly in love with him. If it wasn't for Charlotte, he wondered whether he would have stayed, some days – but then he'd catch a glimpse of Gina smiling as she read, or see her frowning as she stared at the computer, and his heart would leap.

'I'm sorry, love, but I need to pop out for a minute.'

Gina rolled her eyes. 'But you promised. How am I supposed to write with a toddler who won't sit still?' Gina put her hands on her hips.

'I know, but this is important.' Will moved to kiss her but Gina moved her head away. 'Don't try to mollycoddle me,' she grumbled, before stomping to the range.

Will smiled. She'd be more than mollycoddled when he returned.

Gina let the curtains fall from the window. Where on earth was he? Hamish hadn't seen him and Mrs Leavers wasn't aware he had any meetings today. A flash of anger seared through her. He wasn't with someone else, was he? She stalked to the phone and dialled his number again. 'Will, where the hell are you? I am really worried now.' She looked over at Charlotte, whose little face turned up to hers, lips pouted, and softened her voice. 'Please call me.'

She hung up, just as the doorbell rang. 'See? Daddy's back now.' Charlotte toddled towards the door, and Gina took her hand, picking her up after a few small steps. They'd be there for ten minutes, otherwise.

A genuine smile spread across her face, but faded as she took in the police uniforms.

'Mrs Lockwood?'

Gina gripped the door. 'Yes,' she said, her body shaking.

'I'm Constable Collins, and this is Constable Ashton. May we come inside?'

Gina nodded, ushering them into the hall.

Constable Collins held out a cup of tea to her, and her left hand trembled, splashing the tea on to the saucer. She put the cup down, looking towards the ceiling. Constable Ashton had taken Charlotte to do some drawing, thank goodness. Although how she would tell her Will wasn't coming home, she didn't want to think about.

'He didn't suffer, he would have passed as soon as the other car hit him,' Constable Ashton said in a quiet voice.

Gina nodded, her body numb. 'That's good,' she heard herself saying.

Good? What was she saying?

The police officer gave her a grim smile. 'We found this amongst his belongings,' she said, pulling a box out of her pocket and placing it in Gina's hands. 'He was on the way back from the jewellers, it seems.'

A lump rose in Gina's throat. *Jewellers. And I thought he was with another woman.* She shook her head. *I'd rather him be cheating and alive though, than this,* she thought, prising the box open.

She gasped at the sight: a diamond eternity ring, gleaming so brightly she frowned at it. *And the last thing I did was give him attitude. I didn't even kiss him before he left.*

Gina let out a sob.

She would never see him coming through the door again; with his happy-go-lucky smile and ruffled hair. Never see him coaxing a smile out of Charlotte when she was tetchy. And he would never coax another smile out of her.

Spots formed in her eyes, and she blinked as the blackness filled her vision.

'Mrs Lockwood?' The last thing she felt was her head tilting forward, and Constable Collins grabbing her by the shoulders.

Chapter Fifty Six

'It was riveting,' Harriet said, patting the manuscript on her desk. 'I read it from start to finish in one sitting.'

Gina nodded, her lips parting in a small smile. Writing her story had been a comfort, distraction, and catharsis. Pouring her own guilt, shame and fears into something that would help others had drawn her from her catatonic grief, but seeing her story in print was a confronting moment. There it was, in black and white: she'd tried to find love by ignoring what her heart told her, and she'd hurt two men in the process. She was lucky, despite her mistakes, to have been blessed with Charlotte.

During the nights when guilt haunted her, she would gaze at her sleeping daughter and give thanks for her most precious gift; and hope that someday, she might find peace.

'Will you reconsider *The List*?' Harriet asked, raising her eyebrows.

Gina shook her head. 'No, I'm done with lists,' she replied. 'From now on,' she said, tapping her heart and looking down at Charlotte, 'this dictates what I do.'

As if on cue, Charlotte reached out and grabbed a shiny glass paperweight from Harriet's desk.

'That's Tiffany's, sweetheart, now give it back to Aunty Harriet,' Harriet coaxed, springing from behind the desk with a rapidity that belied her glossy appearance.

'We'll leave Aunty Harriet now.' Gina laughed and pried the paperweight from Charlotte's hands, before sitting her in the buggy.

'Will you stay in Australia?' Harriet asked as she walked them to the lift.

'No. Will's mother isn't well, so I need to be here for her,' she said quietly. As much as she wanted to escape the memories, Charlotte needed her grandmother, and Elly needed them both.

Harriet nodded. 'When you're ready to write again, call me at once.' She pulled Gina into a hug. 'Don't stay away too long.'

Gina nodded, her smile fading as the lift doors closed. She hadn't been able to tell Harriet, but there would be no more books, as well as no more lists. Perhaps she would go back to being a lawyer, and pour her energy into righting the wrongs suffered by others. She sighed. *I'll think about that later.*

It had become her new motto – after years of planning, then fretting when things didn't work out, she'd discovered the joy of letting life unfold. It wasn't feasible to live without a plan forever, she knew; but for now, her plan was to get through each day as a good mum. The rest would come.

She glanced at her watch. Four hours before their flight. Plenty of time.

'Mama, I want Iggle.'

Gina reached into her handbag. 'Yes, here you are.' She pulled out the small toy, brushed it again to ensure it didn't have any dirt from the floor of Harriet's office, and handed it to Charlotte.

Things were going smoothly, too smoothly . . . She frowned. The handbag seemed emptier than it had at home . . . She pulled it open, her heart sinking as she noticed her travel wallet missing. 'Oh you've got to be joking', she said, closing her eyes. She'd put it on the hall table as they left, because Charlotte had run out the door with no shoes on . . .

She sighed. That child would run bare foot into the snow if you let her, cold temperatures didn't bother her in the slightest.

'We have to go home darling, Mummy forgot our tickets.'

Charlotte giggled. 'Mummy silly.' She turned in her buggy and looked up at her, putting her hands over her mouth. Silly was word she'd be chastised for saying to her mother, but it was hard to disagree in the circumstances.

'You're not wrong there, sweetie,' Gina mumbled, before pushing the buggy out the open lift doors.

Sean hurried into the station to catch the train to Manchester, weaving between passengers on the busy platform with a smile. He used to hate crowds, but now, they were a reminder of his freedom.

And hopefully, his future.

He had clung to the memory of Gina during his captivity, every day strengthening his resolve. He'd failed to fight for her before. He vowed that if he was freed, he would let Gina know that he would do anything, go anywhere, to be with her.

After his rescue and some time in hospital, he had called Harriet to arrange a meeting. That's when he heard about Will's passing.

He'd vacillated, haunted by the thought of Gina grieving on her own, and the possibility she would consider his overture unwelcome.

Then when he read the book, he knew.

A deep resonating chime broke, drawing his eyes to the old-fashioned station clock. *Maybe I'll buy her a grandfather clock,* he thought with a smile. *A symbol of all the time in our future.*

Four hours later he stood outside Gina's house, rehearsing his opening line again. He'd had years to craft it, but now the moment had arrived, his mouth was dry, and his mind blank.

Unbelievable. Sean sighed. *Well, I can't just stand here.*

But I can't stand on the doorstep grinning silently, either.

He frowned, hoping the neighbours weren't watching; then he heard a bump, followed by something crashing to the floor.

His mouth stretched into a grin, and he reached up and pressed the bell.

Chapter Fifty Seven

Gina placed the flowers on the gravestone as Charlotte kissed it. 'Love you,' Charlotte said as she stroked the marble.

Tears stung at the corners of Gina's eyes. She avoided coming here, but Sean had insisted. Between him and Charlotte she'd been forced to walk into her crucible and face the years of shame, guilt and blame she'd allowed to direct her path. It was a slow process, and she'd stumbled many times. In the early days, she had reverted back to her usual pattern, insisting that Sean leave her and Charlotte to take up a promotion in Port Moresby. He'd ignored her and settled for a less interesting job in the High Commission in London until Charlotte was older, so Elly could see her grow up. Poor Elly had been too heartbroken by Will's passing, dying a year later. Her passing was another piece of emotional baggage Gina had been carrying.

Guilt had become such a familiar companion that she had felt almost naked without it, stubbornly clawing for it to cloak her in its stealthy, parasitic folds. As she was about to accept it around her shoulders once more, Sean touched her hand, and Charlotte took the other.

No. Instead she would accept a cloak which had forgiveness, love and hope woven into every stitch.

Epilogue

'I don't know how you get any work done,' sighed Harriet. 'Living in the Pacific and taking sailing holidays seems rather decadent. I need to pay my authors less in future. Or at least organise a visit to them.'

Gina laughed. 'After years living in the UK I've earned this sunshine.'

'Hmmph. Don't stay away forever though.'

Charlotte smiled. 'We won't. Sean's next posting orders come through soon. After living in PNG, I hope it's not somewhere too cold.'

She ended the call and glanced out the window at the aquamarine water. It was a decadent life, living with the man she loved, and her beautiful daughter. As if that wasn't enough, she'd become a well-respected author. In every book she wrote, she channelled the pain of her journey; and to her surprise, women responded to that more than the exotic settings or the gripping storylines.

Some good had come of it all, in the end.

Sean bounded down the steps from the deck, tanned torso glistening, and Gina grinned as she admired his well-defined abs. Perhaps good was an understatement.

'Looking good there, gorgeous,' he said, winking.

Gina laughed, a sound she'd grown used to living her list-less life. 'You're not looking too bad yourself,' she replied, winking back.

The End

Other Books by Darcy Delany

Love Gone Wrong:
Short stories about love and all its debacles

Sweet Revenge: Sometimes Karma Needs a Little Help

I Don't Date in December:
The Modern Day Fairy Tale Series- Book One

The Go-Between:
The Modern Day Fairy Tale Series Book Two

If you'd like exclusive sneak peeks of Darcy's future releases, sign up to *Sassy Snippets* on her Facebook page:

https://www.facebook.com/darcydelanyauthor

About the Author

Darcy Delany writes contemporary romance, chick lit, science fiction and historical fiction featuring strong, sassy and quirky heroines.

Darcy loves history, fabulous food and old movies. A fan of British home shows, Darcy dreams of one day restoring a Georgian mansion; if she can pay contractors to do all the hard work for her.